Fr

FRANK AND DALIA

A Chance Encounter

A Novel

James A. LaMonica

iUniverse, Inc.

New York Lincoln Shanghai

Frank and Dalia
A Chance Encounter

iUniverse books may be ordered through booksellers or by contacting:

iUniverse
2021 Pine Lake Road, Suite 100
Lincoln, NE 68512
www.iuniverse.com
1-800-Authors (1-800-288-4677)

Because of the dynamic nature of the Internet, any Web addresses
or links contained in this book may have changed
since publication and may no longer be valid.

This is a work of fiction. All of the characters, names, incidents,
organizations, and dialogue in this novel are either the products of the
author's imagination or are used fictitiously.

ISBN: 978-0-595-42239-5 (pbk)
ISBN: 978-0-595-86577-2 (ebk)

Printed in the United States of America

This book is dedicated to all the people in the world who are or have been abused and mistreated. There is hope. And to all the people who are able to help, you can. Just reach out. It's easier than you think.

A lot of people unknowingly contributed to this book. By that I mean people I met over the years had characteristics that many of my characters have. The main character, Frank could have been my father, my brother or either one of my brothers-in-law. These are people who help others for no apparent reason except they want to make another person's life a little better, even if for just a little while.

Thank you to the very few "first readers". Your comments were not only encouraging but helpful.

A special thank you to my niece Ann who was always able to help me find the right word or phrase to complete the thought. I'll always treasure the times we spent together just talking not only about the story but everything else. Her knowledge and expertise were invaluable in the completion of the book. I know there were times when it wasn't easy for her to meet with me and I'm sure that her family made some sacrifices too. For this I will always be grateful to Ann and her family.

Finally to my wife who encouraged me all the way. She always knew when to say something and when not to. A thank you for letting the manuscript accompany us on several road trips where we read and re-read the story to make sure we got it right. I hope we did.

PROLOGUE

▼

Sharon had looked for Dalia for more than a year now. Here she was outside the flower shop that Dalia managed, but hesitated to go in. What will she say to me? Will she even recognize me? They said she was a completely different person than the one two years ago. So much has happened in such a short time, Sharon thought.

Last week when Sharon first came by, Dalia was at the suppliers buying flowers for the upcoming Mother's Day weekend. "I knew this was a bad time," Sharon muttered to herself. The owner, Stanley Benson, was in the shop and overheard Sharon. He told her what a lifesaver Dalia was. He went on to explain that if it wasn't for her, he would have had to close the shop. He wasn't sure at the time if she would work out, but there was something about her, so he gave Dalia a chance.

"She turned out to be the best thing that could've happened to me," Stanley said. Despite the fact that she had no formal training in horticulture, she had a natural ability for mixing and arranging flowers. She had told him it was something she had picked up many years ago from her aunt. "Personally, I don't know what I'd do without her."

Stanley lived in the house adjacent to the shop and Dalia was basically the caretaker for her aging boss. He told Sharon that Dalia cared for him like a daughter would care for her father, and he never took her for granted.

Finally Sharon walked in. Dalia was in the back room when she heard the jingle of the front door bells. She walked out, wiping her hands on her apron. As soon as she saw Sharon, she got a terrible feeling in the pit of her stomach. Her expression changed and immediately she wanted to run and go hide in the back room.

Neither woman spoke. Dalia stared at her feet. Slowly Sharon moved forward and extended a tentative hand. Then she took Dalia's hand and both women embraced. They both sobbed, cradled in each other's arms.

Sharon told Dalia that she has been looking for her for some time. Dalia said she was unable to face her or the rest of the family.

"I'm so sorry things turned out the way they did," Dalia said. "I never expected Frank to come back so soon that morning. If he waited for just a few minutes, I would've been gone and out of his life forever."

"Dalia," Sharon said, "you never would have been out of my father's life. You were too important to him. He would've found you one way or another. I knew that my father cared for you. I wasn't too sure how much you cared for him, to be honest. Then I found the letter you left for him that morning. After reading it, I realized what you did was because you loved him so much, you didn't want anything to happen to him. What you didn't realize, Dalia, that at the time my father loved you so much, he wasn't going to allow anything to happen to you. After my father got to know you, I began to see a change. He had a purpose, and the purpose was you. He was happy with you, Dalia, and his life felt complete again." Then Sharon reached into her handbag and took out a small, velvet gift box. She handed it to Dalia and said, "My mother always wore this locket. My mother told me that it was a gift from my father when he first went off to school. It wasn't the most expensive piece of jewelry he ever gave her, but she cherished it. After she died, we couldn't find it, and figured it must have been lost going back and forth to the hospital. Well, I found it in one of Dad's bureau drawers. Dalia, I know he wanted you to have it." Sharon handed the locket to Dalia. When she opened it she saw Frank's and her pictures. Seeing the expression on Dalia's face, Sharon gently took the other woman's hand and said, "Stay in touch. I think my father wanted you to be a part of his family."

Driving back to Rochester, Sharon's thoughts drifted back to the time before Dalia entered her father's life.

CHAPTER 1

▼

Frank Noble settled into his lifestyle. Laura had been gone for over four years now. He had his routine, a small circle of friends, and his family. Frank was still too young to retire, but when Mid Plains Life was outbid by the much larger Consolidated Life Insurance of America (CL), it was just a matter of time before management would "trim the fat."

Frank worked for Mid Plains for over thirty years. He started in debit sales and climbed to regional sales manager for the northeast territory. Frank was a gifted salesman and natural leader. He could open a territory with fewer men than any of his colleagues, and knew how to get the most out of his people. Frank led by example, teaching his workers to be fair and honest with all customers, not just those seeking large policies. No account was too small to get Frank's attention and best effort. He insisted his salesmen do it that way too, simply because that was the only way to do business. Frank was respected, not only by his men and top management at Mid Plains, but by the competition as well. Over the years, Frank turned down several job offers from outside companies because of his unwavering loyalty to the company that first gave him his start in a business he had grown to love.

It wasn't long after CL bought the Company that things started to change. The most important aspect of the job now was the "bottom line." Salesmen were discouraged from spending too much time with customers in lower income brackets. They had quotas to meet on a weekly basis. The pressure was on and morale was low.

It was at this time that Laura, his wife, became ill. Frank was able to take time off because he had qualified and trust-worthy staff to take over while he was gone. What became his first priority was Laura's health. Frank sought out the best doctors and treatment for his wife, no matter where it took him.

*   *   *   *

Laura was the only woman Frank ever loved. They met the summer after graduation, just before he went to college, intro-duced by mutual friends. Frank was mesmerized with Laura's stunning beauty. Deep auburn hair, sapphire blue eyes, and a sunset glowing complexion. At first it was just a group of friends hanging out, kids planning and anticipating what they'd be doing after school, their futures. Before long, how-ever, Frank and Laura knew they were destined to be together. It might have been the innocence of the late 1950s, when life was much less complicated, carefree and wonderful, a special and unique time to start a love affair that for Frank and Laura would last a lifetime. Frank's first year away at college was not only difficult because of his academics, but because he missed Laura so much.

Frank and Laura were married the summer after his first year at Penn State. He then transferred to a local college so Laura could work while he finished school. By the time Frank started his third year, Laura was pregnant with their first child. Times were difficult for them, and neither anticipated the struggle of supporting a small family. So when it came time for Frank to start his last year, he decided it would be best to find a job and finish his education later.

The years up until Laura became ill were the happiest of their lives. Frank climbed the corporate ladder at his job. They had four children; Laura was active in community and church affairs, and even managed to open a small gift shop of her own. Their two sons and two daughters were independent and successful in their respective careers. Frank jr. was married with two children and lived nearby. Ken had taken a job with a computer company and lived in the affluent part of down-state New York, just north of Manhattan with his wife and three young sons. Their third daughter, Carol, married well, and had twin girls and a boy, also in town. Sharon, their youngest, lived in Rochester, and worked for an advertising agency. She had dreams of becoming a famous novelist, which Frank always encouraged.

Like any large family growing up, they had their ups and downs. But through all the trials and tribulations, Frank and Laura always kept their special love affair strong, like an ever burning candle. They were each other's best friend. Often when Frank struggled with a business decision, Laura listened patiently while he discussed the pros and cons, sometimes for hours, sometimes for days. When he finally came to a decision, he'd always thank her, even if she never said a word. It was his way of expressing his appreciation. Simply her presence brought him peace of mind.

When Laura wanted to start a business of her own, Frank supported her every step of the way. Even when she had doubts about her ability, timing, location and all the other things she thought could go wrong. Frank guided her, saw her through the tiniest of details. He was her champion. You couldn't find two people more in tune with each other than Frank and Laura.

Her sickness blindsided them and took over their lives. They just returned from an extended vacation to Europe, a trip they thoroughly enjoyed beyond belief. Their children greeted them at the airport upon their return home. Friends and relatives also showed up to listen to all the stories of their adventures and encounters with the people they met. They ate, laughed, and drank until the wee hours of the night, finally settling into bed to recount their stories again to each other, and remark how truly blessed they were and how good life was. They had a beautiful family, many good friends and such good fortune. Little did they know that this would be the end of their life together as they knew it.

At first Laura thought her condition was the result of jet lag or the rich diet she had during vacation. However, after her initial visit to their family doctor and several trips to one specialist after another, their worst fears became reality. The prognosis was between six months and a year to live.

CHAPTER 2

▼

Dalia Preston had trouble producing for her pimp. She was more dependent on drugs now than she had ever been. It was a vicious cycle. She had to work more to satisfy her habit. Trouble was dope was a downer. It shut down the whole central nervous system, making its user listless and numb, the feeling Dalia craved. But the hours and the lack of sleep caught up to her. Although she had always been a pretty woman with almond shaped hazel eyes, high cheekbones, and chestnut skin, the drugs and her lifestyle took its toll. Baxter was not only her pimp, but also her supplier. He would charge her top dollar for her dope and then cut it down so that she needed it more often. He gave her so little money she could barely live. The night Dalia stopped to get something to eat before she went home, her usual routine, Baxter beat her like he never did before.

It was almost ten o'clock and Dalia had only been with two johns. The last one refused to pay her the thirty dollars they agreed on, because he said she did not complete the job. She dreaded going to see Baxter at the "Fox Club," but there was no way she was going to last the night. She thought if she had some food, she'd feel better. Then again, Dalia knew the only thing that would help her at this point was another fix. Seeing Baxter was her only choice. How could she convince him to give her a fix now and she'd promise to make it up to him later. She knew that if she went back to the apartment, she'd risk getting a beating showing up with so little cash. Her body couldn't take another pounding from Baxter, Dalia thought. She decided to stay out a bit longer.

A half-hour later she went back to the apartment hoping she'd be alone. If she could only get something to eat and some sleep, she knew she'd feel better the next day.

When Dalia entered the cluttered, cramped, studio on East Main Street, the smell along with the wrappers and remnants of the last few meals, reminded her of her desperate state. Old newspapers and magazines were scattered close to the only overflowing trash pail in the corner. She moved some dirty clothes and used plastic bags from the bed, wishing to fall asleep before the pain in her head and the gnawing in her stomach became unbearable. She barely closed her eyes when she heard the unmistakable pounding of Baxter coming up the stairs.

He opened the door, gazed around the room and went right to the cigar box on the mantel where Dalia put her nightly wages.

"What's this, girl? You've been out all night and you bring me this?" Baxter shouted, crumpling the few bills in his hands.

"Baxter, honey, I had to get something to eat, sweetheart. That cheap bastard only gave me fifteen dollars after he agreed to pay me fifty. Then the man at the diner gypped me out of my change. Baxter, just help me a little, man," Dalia pleaded. "I'll make it up to you, I swear, you know I will. I always do. Just help me now, please," she begged, her voice trailing off.

"Shit, woman, you make me sick, bitch. I always treated you special. And this is the thanks I get?" He threw the crumpled bills on the floor. Then Baxter tenderly helped Dalia up from her bed with his left hand, and in the next instant brought his right hand across the side of her head. SMACK. After several blows to her head, Baxter completed his assault and pushed her out the door and down the stairs. Dalia staggered a few feet and collapsed in a doorway. Now she would get the rest she so desperately needed.

Dalia couldn't stomach another beating. Baxter's anger and blows were getting more severe each time. Many times after she thought it would be best if Baxter killed her, at least she'd be out of her misery. Dalia knew that she wouldn't be with Baxter much longer. It was common knowledge that when your pimp marked up your face, he was done with you. The face was the key, not so much the arrangement of the eyes, nose and mouth, but the expression of the eyes. A woman's eyes held the truth, and either brought a man to his knees or left him feeling lost. Dalia's held the former.

This time Baxter not only slapped her on the cheek several times, but also punched her face, bruising her cheek, eye, and splitting her lip. She knew this was a warning. If she didn't produce, the next time he'd use his closed fists, and beat her face like a drum, 'till she dropped. Dalia knew she had to quit first before he quit her. Working for Baxter was not an ideal situation, but on the streets alone was worse. In this neighborhood the girls who worked alone, eventually ended up in some alley dead, either overdosed, beaten by an unsatisfied customer, or a new gang member who had to prove something to be initiated.

Dalia was at the lowest point in her life. She couldn't imagine sinking deeper. That night she was gyped by an unsatisfied john, short-changed at the diner and beaten about the face by Baxter.

When a man approached her and wanted to help, Dalia lashed out at him because all she saw was another man, who wanted to take advantage of her, like all the men in her life since she was a little girl.

Dalia never knew her real father. The men in the foster homes she lived in had almost always abused her. By the time she was thirteen, she had experienced every kind of abuse: physical, psychological, verbal, sexual. When the police officer showed up, Dalia made it seem like this man had beaten her. He was the man that would *pay* for all the abuse she had suffered in her life.

*   *   *   *

It was unseasonably warm in western New York that late March night. Rochester was not a hot bed of jazz, like some of the larger cities, but if you wanted to hear good music, you could visit one of the small clubs in the downtown area. Frank planned to meet his friend, Tom Dutton, and see "The Tee Jay Trio" at the C-Note Bar and Grill.

As Frank dressed that night to meet Tom, he started to talk out loud to his wife's framed picture on the nightstand. "Don't worry, I'm just meeting Tom for something to eat and then listen to a little jazz. Do you think this shirt is okay?" He posed in front of the full-length mirror behind the bedroom door. "Of course it is. I knew you would like it." He chuckled, "I'd like to take you with me, but I don't think you would like the group. Of course, if you were really here, we would go somewhere else, maybe a movie or the theatre. On second thought, we'd go dancing! Oh, how we loved to dance. And what good dancers we were, a perfect match." Frank put one arm across his waist and another in the air, made believe he was holding Laura. "I'd give anything to dance with you again. Oh, well, another time, dear. I have to get going if I want to be on time. Don't worry, I won't be late. See you later," he said and blew a kiss to his wife.

Frank and Tom had known each other for many years. They worked together at Mid Plains Life. Tom was too young for an early retirement, so had taken over Frank's position at Consolidated Life. They both liked the same kind of music, and enjoyed each other's company. They had a late supper and listened to the first set.

When it was time to go, Tom reminded Frank to be careful walking to the car. The city was doing it's best to clean up the downtown neighborhood, but there were still some unsavory parts in town, if not downright dangerous. Frank, however, was not concerned for his safety at all, since his car was parked around the corner from the main street, which was always well lit.

As Frank approached his car, he thought he heard a moan coming from a darkened storefront doorway across the street. He could barely make out the figure in the doorway, but on closer examination, he could see a person slumped over and moaning. He crossed the street, and as he drew nearer, he asked if he could help. As the figure turned toward him, he saw it was a woman who appeared to have been beaten. Immediately Frank took out his cell phone to call 911.

Dalia was in no mood for some jerk to get involved. As soon as she heard the beep of the cell phone, she swung her arm towards Frank and knocked the device out of his hands, against the doorway and down into her lap. Frank, completely taken aback by Dalia's reaction, bent down and searched for his phone. Dalia confused and angry that this guy would not go away, started hitting him about his back and shoulders. It was dark and Frank was getting worried now, when a police cruiser pulled up.

"Can I help you, sir," one officer said abruptly. He grabbed Frank and threw him against the car. He held him there while he called for back up on his two-way. With Dalia's shouting for Frank to leave her alone, naturally the officer assumed it was Frank who had beaten her. Before he knew it, Frank was handcuffed and sitting it the back of the cruiser, headed for the station.

"There's where I found the woman, in the doorway," Frank insisted to the police. "She was already beaten."

"Then why did the lady say it was you who beat her? Huh? You're going to headquarters, buddy, so shut up," was all the cop had to say. Once they got there, he was processed, finger-printed, and treated like a criminal.

When the ambulance crew arrived, they examined Dalia and determined that her injuries were not serious enough for an emergency room. After her wounds were dressed, she was also taken down to headquarters for questioning.

Frank insisted that he did not beat Dalia. "I was just trying to help, officer, you've got to believe that, and I can't explain why she would accuse me of beating her."

Frank's story checked out.

"Okay, Mr. Noble, we'll release you on your own recognizance, but you still have to appear pending Dalia's statement," the desk officer said.

While Frank was telling his story at headquarters, one of his customers, Ray Sanders, a police sergeant, spotted him and went over to see if he could help.

"Hey, Frank, can I be of some service? Fellas, can you treat this guy with a little respect? Fellas?" Ray said, lowering his voice with disappointment. "I'll see what I can do, Frank." I know you didn't do anything wrong."

"Thanks, Ray, I owe you one. Really, thank you so much," Frank said, shaking off his shirt and wiping his trousers, like he was ridding himself of the disgrace. As Frank headed toward the Exit sign, he saw Dalia. Their eyes met, locked for a moment, and then she turned away. He saw eyes full of anger, despair, hopelessness and bitterness. Frank could not sleep that night. He could not get out of this head that haunting look on Dalia's face. He wondered why she blamed *him* for her beating. Why get *him* in trouble? Whenever he closed his eyes, all he saw was that look. It troubled and saddened him at the same time.

*   *   *   *

The next day his family came to visit. They wanted to hear about his ordeal the night before. Later, Tom Dutton stopped by and teased him about the "hooker" that got him in trouble. At first Frank laughed it off, but when everyone left, and he was alone, he thought about Dalia, and that look on her face could not escape him. It bothered him so much the rest of the day, he decided he had to find out more about this woman, Dalia.

Frank went back to the police station the next day, and inquired whether Dalia was still being held there. The desk sergeant remarked that she must be in trouble since her "pimp" hadn't even bailed her out yet.

"What will happen to her?" Frank asked.

"Well, if no one bails her out, she'll have to stay here a few more days, then we have to let her go," the officer said. "And it isn't going to be pretty, if you know what I mean," he smiled, obnoxiously. Frank looked puzzled. "She's a dope addict. Withdrawal is very painful."

"Can I bail her out," Frank asked.

"Mr. Noble," the sergeant laughed, "go home and forget it. This is another world, these people are hopeless." Frank could hear him still laughing as he slowly walked out of the station.

There must be a way to help, he thought when he got home and did some yard work and other chores, trying to get his

mind off Dalia and that look on her face when he was leaving
the station two days ago. That look haunted him. Later, while
eating supper, he suddenly realized where he had seen that
look before. He saw that same look on Laura's beautiful face
when she got sick. For the first time in a long time, Frank put
his head down into his folded arms on the table, and sobbed.

Frank went again the next day to the station, determined to
do something and get Dalia released, but instead found out
that she had been sent to the hospital because of a suicide
attempt. When he went to the hospital, the nurses wouldn't
let him see her because of her serious condition.

"Why don't you call in a few days to see if her condition
changes," the nurse at the front desk suggested to him. As
Frank left the hospital, the memory of what he went through
with Laura came back. He couldn't help but think that even
though Laura and Dalia had very little in common, their situations were similar. Both were hopeless. Both had a hold on
Frank that he knew the reasons with Laura, but he was unsure
of with Dalia. Then he got to thinking, and realized that
Laura's illness *was hopeless*.

Dalia, on the other hand, didn't have to be. There was
nothing Frank could have done to make Laura well, but there
must be something he could do for Dalia.

CHAPTER 3

▼

Frank went back to the hospital the next day and demanded to know who was handling Dalia's case. After giving him the run-a-round, one of the nurses sent him to Westfall Agency that did follow up with abandoned patients, or patients like Dalia who needed drug rehabilitation. After waiting what seemed like hours, Frank was sent to a Ms. Maria Vargas, a very busy woman and difficult to connect with. When he finally did, Maria was able to arrange a meeting with Frank.

Maria Vargas worked for Westfall Agency for almost twenty years. She had seen thousands of cases, and the names and faces ran together and were very hard for her to keep track of, let alone remember.

"Who are you?" Maria asked Frank. "And why, sir, are you so interested in this Dalia person?"

Frank tried to explain who he was and how he and Dalia met. Frank could see the puzzled look on Maria's face as he was talking.

"Why, sir, can I ask again, do you want to help this woman?" Maria asked. Frank evaded the question, and asked another.

"Where will Dalia go when she is released from the hospital?"

"Probably Baxter," Maria answered bluntly. "And who knows how long he'll keep her."

"Who's Baxter?" Frank asked.

"Honey, a woman like Dalia has only one person who would care for her and it's only for what he can get out of her, and that one person is her pimp."

"That's it?" Frank was astonished. "And you would release her to her pimp?"

"Me? Yes, Frank, because I have no choice. For every person working in this agency there are a hundred Dalias, no, a thousand Dalias, hell, there's probably ten thousand Dalias. How do I know? Hell, all I know is every morning when I come to work, there's a list on my desk with about twenty cases that I have to manage. They call it case management. If I see three, I'm lucky. Do you know what that means, Frank? Tomorrow there's twenty more plus the seventeen I didn't see today. You do the math, Frank. Yes, I'll turn her over to her pimp, and I'll try not to let it bother me. And if I'm lucky, it won't bother me, not at all…. .say, until maybe a week or a month later, or whenever a colleague will tell me, 'Maria, remember so and so, that case you were working on? What a shame, they found her in a dumpster.' That's my life here, Frank." Maria sighed heavily and folded her hands across her desk, sat upright, pulled her head back. "So, now, Frank, what can I do for you?"

"I'm sorry, Ms. Vargas. I guess I'm out of line"

"Yeah, I might say, a bit."

"Let's start over, okay."

"Sure, Frank, I like you. I'm a social worker. I know the genuine article when I see it."

Maria told Frank that Dalia's case was not unique, except for the fact that she had absolutely no one, no friends, no family, no one. Maria went over to the filing cabinet in her cluttered office, pulled out a file and began reading.

"When Dalia Preston was four-years-old, her mother was hit by a car and she died a short time after. It seemed no one knew who her father was, and that is why she has her mother's last name. Because her grandmother had young children of her own, Dalia was put into foster care. By the time she was about five or six, she had been in five different foster homes. And then an interesting thing happened," Maria commented, "at the age of six, a Mrs. Robinson took her and we lost track of her for about a year and a half after that." Maria put down the file, looked up at Frank, "There's nothing in this report about that time. But apparently, according to Dalia, that was a very happy time for her. Dalia told me about living with her "Aunt Jessie", and her cousin, Carrie. She doesn't know exactly where it was, but she knows it was in the country. Out of all the places she's been, and wherever she goes since, those were the happiest days of her life. I definitely remember her telling me that!"

"What happened then?" Frank asked. "Why did she leave that place?"

"Well, according to Dalia, she remembers coming home from school with her cousin, playing, skipping and laughing like kids do, having so much fun, not bothered about anything, and as they got closer to Aunt Jessie's house, they saw the fire trucks. One of her aunt's friends came running up to the girls, and took them to her house, even though they wanted to see their aunt. It appears that there was a fire at Aunt Jessie's house. She didn't survive it."

"Those poor kids," Frank shook his head.

"The two girls wondered what would happen to them. For a few days they clung to each other and said no matter what, they would always stay together. In a few days, however, after Aunt Jessie was buried, a lady came for Dalia, and brought her back to another foster home. She would never see her cousin Carrie again.

She has absolutely no way of knowing where her cousin is, and she often dreams of those happy times that she shared with Carrie. She wonders how Carrie's life has turned out. She wants to know how Carrie is, but doesn't want Carrie to know anything about her life."

"Isn't there anything else in that file about her aunt or cousin or where in the country they lived for that short time?" Frank asked, deeply concerned.

"Frank, you've got to understand, sometimes records get lost, some agencies don't keep records like we do around here, especially now," Maria said, trying to be helpful. She went back to reading the file. "More foster homes, problems in school, running away, picked up for prostitution the first time at thirteen-years-old. Her foster father's brother was pimping her." She stopped, looked at Frank, "Should I read on, Frank, or have you had enough?" Maria looked at her watch. "I have to get going, I've already given you too much of my time, not to mention too much information."

Frank was puzzled. He couldn't believe what he just heard. He knew Dalia must have had a tough life, that part was not unbelievable. But forced into prostitution at thirteen-years-old? "Hell, I've got a granddaughter almost that age," he said out loud.

As Maria Vargas showed Frank to the door, she thought to herself, what a nice guy, but she'd probably never see him again

*   *   *   *

Frank tried to sleep that night, but the circumstances of Dalia's childhood swirled in his head. He kept thinking that there had to be something he could do, must do. Dalia's pain and suffering were dominating his thoughts. At one time when he looked up in the middle of the night, he turned toward Laura's picture, and said, "Laura, what shall I do? The look on that poor woman's face, her mixed up childhood, the suicide attempt. Laura, there must be something I could do, but what? What? If you were here, I know you would have an answer. You always knew the right thing to do." Finally, he drifted off.

*   *   *   *

Tom Dutton's call woke him up the next morning.

"Hey, buddy, did you over sleep? It's Thursday morning, remember breakfast?"

Frank looked at his watch. "I'll be there shortly."

Frank figured if he met Tom maybe he'd get Dalia off his mind, after all, what could he do for her? And if he did decide to do something, would she even accept his help? That would be a challenge, he thought, and what about her pimp? Would this Baxter guy be a problem?

Frank was glad to see Tom and apologized for being late. They started right off talking about things at Consolidated Life Frank enjoyed these weekly meetings. They discussed business trends, politics, sports, just about everything under the sun. Frank liked that he and Tom had become closer since Laura died. Even though his friend was a few years younger than Frank, Tom looked up to him. Frank was always like Tom's big brother. They had a lot in common, despite the fact that Tom had two failed marriages and his two children from his first marriage didn't speak to him. He didn't have any children with his second wife, which was just as well since that marriage didn't last long at all. Tom envied Frank because of his close family relationships, and how Frank always put family as his first priority. Tom often told Frank that he wished he had been more of a "family man" when he was younger.

"So Frank, what was going on with the incident the other night with the police and the prostitute?" Tom asked. Frank told Tom that he didn't know why, but it was dominating his thoughts. Tom liked the confidence Frank shared. "You don't think that they'll believe that woman's claim that you beat her, do you, Frank?"

"That's not it, Tom. I just can't understand why that woman became so angry at me. The look on her face that night when I left the station has been haunting me all week. So much so," Frank continued, "that I went down to the station myself, to see if I could do something for her. Turns out, she tried to commit suicide." Tom's mouth dropped. Frank then told Tom about his conversation with the social worker, Maria Vargas, and how Dalia's childhood was, and the fact that she was pimped when she was only thirteen-years-old.

"Sounds bad, Frank, what do you want to do?"

"That's the problem, Tom, I just don't know. I really don't know what to do."

"If I know you, Frank, you'll think of something. Let me know if there's anything I can do to help," Tom said as he patted his friend's back. "You know I'll go the mile for you,"

"Thanks, Tom, I will." Frank smiled and finished his coffee.

While Frank and Tom were just about to finish breakfast, Frank's cell phone rang. It was his daughter-in-law, Shirley, reminding him to come over for dinner tonight to celebrate his granddaughter, Karen's thirteenth birthday. Frank thanked her for the reminder, and realized he had to pick up a gift. These were the times he missed his wife the most. He got angry that he couldn't share these special occasions with her anymore. He had to struggle over what to buy for a birthday gift for a teenager, when Laura would know exactly what the perfect gift was.

Frank and Tom finished their breakfast, said their good-byes, and agreed to meet for a round of golf next week. As Tom walked to his car in the parking lot, he turned around to his friend. "Hey, Frank," he said, "I'm serious about helping you. I know what it feels like to be stuck, not knowing what to do. I'll be there for you, pal."

*   *   *   *

Frank ran some errands and made some mental notes as to what would be an appropriate gift for his teenage granddaughter. With time running short, Frank went to the department store on the way home, where he was bound to see something that would be just right. He passed by a jewelry store on the corner and saw a mannequin in the window wearing a beautiful silver and gold locket around her neck. He stopped and took a closer look. It reminded him of the locket he gave Laura when he first went off to college. Even though it wasn't the most expensive piece of jewelry he ever bought her, Laura treasured it like the crown jewels. After she died, he didn't know what to do with it. He gave some of his wife's possessions to his daughters and daughters-in-law, but for some reason he couldn't part with the locket. Even now he wasn't ready to give it to his granddaughter, Karen. The store was ready to close, so he hurried in and without hesitation bought a similar locket.

As Frank walked back to his car, he wondered if the locket would be an appropriate gift. Wouldn't a thirteen-year-old prefer a new outfit of the latest fashion, or a new electronic device that every teenager must have? Or maybe the latest CD by the most popular teenage heartthrob would be a better gift? Well, it was too late to make any changes now. Frank decided to go home and hoped for the best.

Deep in thought, he hadn't noticed the person he bumped into as he turned the corner on his way to the car. He apologized, not looking up, and continued on his way, when the fellow recognized him. It was Sergeant Ray Saunders, from the police station who helped Frank get released the night he was arrested.

"Hey, Frank, did you hear what happened to that bitch who tried to get you in trouble that night? She tried to off herself," as Ray moved his finger across his neck in a cutting motion.

"Huh?" Frank said, confused.

"Yeah," Ray continued, "Just as well, nobody would miss her anyway. It just saves the taxpayers money," he laughed.

"Oh, yeah," Frank said, wanting only to get to his car. Finally, he sat in his car, angry with himself for not saying anything to Ray about his remarks. But what could be say? Besides, he really didn't have time for a conversation, it happened so fast, and he was surprised at Ray's attitude. Still, he should've said something. Was his silence a sign of agreement with Ray? Damn it, he thought, he should've said something! He should've spoken up, said that he didn't think that way.

Too late for that now. He'd better get home, find a photo for the locket, wrap it and get over to Frank Jr's house for supper.

*   *   *   *

Frank enjoyed these family get-togethers. Laura started them a few years before she died. It helped to stay connected with their growing family. With everybody's busy schedules, the family seemed to drift apart. Laura decided that she'd set aside at least one day a month for everyone to have dinner at Grandpa and Grandma's house. These casual family dinners became an event, which everyone looked forward to. Aunts, uncles, cousins, brothers and sisters visited, ate, exchanged news and overall had a great time joking, laughing, and even dancing. Frank and Laura truly liked the company of his children and grandchildren. Tonight was extra special because it was Karen's thirteenth birthday. Of course, the only one missing was Laura. She would've been so proud of Karen. She had grown up to be a beautiful, responsible young lady. She babysat for her younger siblings and kept her grades up at school. Laura and Karen had a special relationship. Laura loved to spend time with her, take her on shopping trips and stop for lunch at a fancy restaurant. Sometimes they spent the whole day together baking, sewing, working in the flower garden, that Laura loved so much, or just lazing around the house watching movies and having tea. Karen followed her grandmother around the house like they were attached. She imitated whatever Laura did.

Frank found the perfect photo for the locket. It was taken at Karen's christening, and Laura seemed to glow in that picture. Frank still wondered about his choice of a gift, but hoped Karen would be pleased, which she was as soon as she opened the small velvet hinged box. Karen gasped and clutched it to her chest.

"Oh, Grandpa, it's beautiful. I don't know what to say," almost in tears.

"Thank you," her mom, Shirley, said, shoving her daughter gently on the shoulders. Sensing Frank was on the verge of tears as well, brought out the cake and began to sing, "Happy Birthday to you."

Frank had a great time, but on the way home started to think again about what Ray Saunders said, and it got him upset that he didn't say anything. He lay in bed, thoughts going through his mind, and the idea that Dalia was forced into prostitution at the tender age of thirteen, the same age as his granddaughter, drove him crazy. Frank got very little sleep that night and vowed he would do something to help Dalia, but still at this time, he didn't know just how.

The first thing Monday morning Frank went down to Maria Vargas' office to convince her he was going to help Dalia. Maria, in a hurry as usual, told Frank that maybe it would be a good idea to talk to Dalia first.

*   *   *   *

Dalia was confused when she woke up in the hospital. She didn't know why she was there. Slowly she began to piece together the events that led up to her going to jail. She remembered being depressed and thinking that she never wanted to go back to the same old life, where she'd get released to Baxter, have him take care of her, promised him that she'd work harder, then start over again with the drugs. Oh, no, she didn't want to get back into the drugs, but did she really have a choice? Drugs were not a cure, but they made her feel okay, even if it was for just a short time. The drugs, Baxter, the men, feeling cheap, dirty, used, and the beatings were just too much. That's why she took the razor blade, the one she always concealed on her, and slit her wrist. But like everything else, she muffed it. It would have been so easy. No one would have missed her. All her problems would be solved.

Fixing the wounds was nothing, compared to the withdrawal from the drugs. If not for the help from the hospital staff, the pain would've been unbearable. Dalia knew she wasn't out of the woods yet. She had nowhere to go, and if Baxter came to release her, it was just a matter of time before she'd be back on the streets working for him.

Maria Vargas was the first to show up at the hospital. She gave Dalia a big hug. Dalia was delighted to see Maria, but ashamed of herself. After all these years, Maria was the only person in the world who genuinely cared for Dalia or showed any interest in her. In the past when Dalia was in trouble, Maria was there to help her get back on her feet. Dalia promised Maria that she'd go to Rehab, do job training, or continue her education. But Dalia never followed through. Instead Dalia fell for the empty promises of Baxter, or some other man, who only wanted Dalia for what they could get out of her. Dalia held Maria close to her and cried, unable to look at her or let go. She wished Maria was her Aunt Jessie from so many years ago, who with just a hug and a kiss, would make everything better.

"Look at me, Dalia," Maria said. "What am I going to do with you? My, oh my, just what am I going to do with you?" Dalia still couldn't look up. Maria told Dalia that she really had to do it this time. "Child, you have to do it! Child, you have to do it because you're *not* a child. You've got to pull yourself together. Hell, that man's going to beat you good next time, and there may be nothing left of you. Why you girls get involved with men like Baxter, I'll never know." Maria pulled Dalia close to her, and said softly, "I guess I do know why." Maria looked at her watch, realized she had a busy schedule and said, "Dalia, I'll be back in a couple of days, don't worry. I'll tell the nurses not to release you to anyone but me." And in a hurry, she started toward the door. Suddenly, she turned, "Has anyone stopped by to see you, Dalia?"

"No, I don't think so. What do you mean?"

"Oh, nothing, child.... .I just thought.... forget it, I'll see you in a couple of days."

Maria was a very attractive woman, light brown skin, beautiful dark eyes and a full figure. She commanded attention whether she walked into a room, or just strolled down the street. Many of her fellow workers and associates had wanted to date her but she didn't want to get involved.

There was one person a few years ago that grabbed her fancy and practically swept her off her feet. Joseph Rolando was an up and coming real estate broker that catered to the Latino community. He was not only becoming successful in his own right but was showing the community that by establishing home ownership and buying property that they would be able to enjoy the "American Dream". Maria and Joseph were a handsome couple and seemed perfect for each other. Joseph's business sometimes kept him at the office late. One night when he missed an agency function Maria, feeling hurt, questioned how come he wasn't able to break away for the special occasion that meant very much to her. He became very angry and upset and verbally and physically abused her. She had never seen this side of him before and got away from him immediately. Right after the incident he apologized and tried in vain to see her. Eventually he stopped calling.

As a child she remembered her father hitting her mother and her siblings as well as herself. As a social worker every day she sees the results of the many women and their children at the hands of any abusive man. She vowed that she would never put herself in that situation.

Sometimes in her loneliness she wonders if she made the right decision by not giving him another chance. She often blames her career for not having the happiness she could've had with Joseph Rolando

Dalia didn't want to disappoint Maria this time, but what could she do? Even if she got a respectable job, and a decent apartment, inevitably, Baxter would find her and make things easy for her to fall right down his trap. He'd convince her that she didn't have to work because he could take care of her, take her to dinner, buy her gifts, love her, and then a few drinks and before long the drugs. There seemed no escape, but she must get away she thought, far away. But how and where? No family, no real friends, no job, no money, how could she possibly do it on her own?

CHAPTER 4

▼

Frank hadn't seen Dalia since that day after the incident. How would she act toward him? Would she remember him, would she turn on him like she did that night she was beaten? How many people would confront their accuser with the idea of wanting to help them? Even though Frank had always thought of himself as being a very capable salesman, able to "close the deal," he was very apprehensive at this moment about meeting Dalia.

On the way to the hospital he stopped by the florist to buy some flowers. As he approached her room, he felt a twinge in his stomach, not unlike the feeling he got as a young salesman making those first sales calls.

Frank entered the room with some hesitation. Dalia looked up from the magazine she was reading, and looked at him kind of puzzled. They both spoke at the same time. Then he handed her the flowers and said, "Here, these are for you."

"Excuse me, sir," she said, "are you sure you have the right room?"

"Are you Dalia?" Frank asked.

"Yes. Who are you?"

"I'm uh… the guy uh, who tried to help you last week, the night you were hurt. My name is Frank," he said as he put his hand out.

"Oh,"she said, kind of flustered. "I don't want any trouble. What are you doing here?"

"I just wanted to see how you're doing," said Frank.

"I'm doing okay, I think," Dalia responded.

Then there was an uncomfortable silence. Frank searched for something to say. Dalia just stared at him, wondered what Frank was going to do next. He said something about the flowers being a special blend and that if they're kept in fresh water they should last a couple of weeks. Dalia nodded her head. Then Frank asked when she was leaving.

"Pretty soon," Dalia answered.

Again Frank felt a loss for something to say. Suddenly a nurse's aid came in and started talking. She had to get the room ready for another patient, and she hoped this next one would be more company for Dalia. "That last one was too sick to be good company for anybody, not even a cat," said the aid, speaking fast. "Poor thing, she could barely open her mouth and had to be moved because she needed special care." She took the flowers from Dalia, who held them tightly in her hands. "These are pretty, and how beautiful they smell." She tipped her nose in the bunch. "I better find something to put them in." She looked over at Frank and winked. "It was awfully nice of your friend to bring you such pretty flowers, and maybe if Dalia is extra nice, her friend might bring a big box of candy, maybe some chocolate that we all could enjoy," she said as she walked out of the room. The woman created such a whirlwind that neither Frank nor Dalia could have said anything while she was in the room. She talked from the time she walked in until the time she left. Frank and Dalia looked at each other and both smiled. Then slowly they broke into laughter.

"What kind of candy do you like, Dalia?" Frank asked, chuckling. "We better find out what kind the aide likes, but she looks as though as likes all kinds of candy." Again, they looked at each other, smiled, then laughed. It was good to see Dalia laugh. Then Frank felt slightly awkward, and he didn't know what to say now. He wanted to ask Dalia if she had a place to stay after she left the hospital, but thought that might appear too forward.

"Well, then," he said, "I just thought I'd stop by to see how you were doing…. So I guess I better be leaving…. so good-by, and I'm glad to see you're feeling better."

"I don't want any trouble," Dalia said again, feeling a little awkward, but not knowing how to deal with it just now. "Thanks for the flowers…. uh, Frank," she said, as she watched him walk away.

*   *   *   *

Frank was in the parking lot when he saw Maria Vargas. Now Frank was embarrassed when Maria approached him and said hello. He was embarrassed because he told Maria he wanted to so something for Dalia, but when he was with her, he never mentioned the idea.

"So, how did it go, Frank?" Maria asked.

"Well, okay, not really, Maria, I was like … well … tongue-tied. An aide was there, and she distracted me and I never even said anything about helping her."

"Frank, do you have a few minutes? I'd like to talk to you."

"Sure, where would you like to talk," Frank answered.

"Let's get a cup of coffee, shall we?" Maria gently put her arm through his elbow and started walking to a nearby diner.

"Frank," she started, leaning close to him over the counter. "I'm worried about Dalia this time. This was a close call. I believe that if nothing is done this time, Dalia won't last another episode with Baxter, or someone like him, you know what I mean?" She took a sip of coffee. Frank was worried. He stared down at his coffee. "Resources are low, Frank, funding is cut, and finding a place for Dalia and a program is going to be more difficult than in the past. Now, listen," Maria looked at him gravely, "you indicated that you wanted to do something, help her out. Well if you're serious, what exactly could you do?"

"I'm serious, Maria," Frank said. "What kind of help are you talking about?"

"Real help, Frank, that's why I want to know if you're sincere. You see, first of all she needs a place to stay, away from the people that use her, off the streets. Second, she has to have some kind of job or be in a job training program, and third, most importantly, more than ever before, she needs to know that someone really is concerned about her. Women like Dalia have no self-esteem, no self-confidence, no self-worth, and the men who take advantage of them and abuse them prey on this fact. Frank, if she doesn't do something to change right now, there won't be a next time for her. She'll become another statistic, I can tell you that. So you tell me this, what can you do?"

With no hesitation, Frank answered, "I'll find her a place to stay, and get her a job, or at least job training. I think, if I do that, she'll know I'm concerned about her."

"It's not that easy, Frank, you won't be the first man who's said he'd help her. Remember, every man she's every known has either abused her or taken advantage of her. Do you think she'll think you're any different?"

"Maria, you have to convince her that I *am* different. You do that and I'll take care of the rest," Frank said, swallowing the last of his coffee.

"Frank, I believe you," Maria said, as she put her coffee mug down, rose from the table and gave Frank a firm handshake. "I'll go talk to her now, and you see what you can do about the apartment and a job. I'll call you tomorrow. And, one more thing, Frank, Thank you."

Instead of going to the hospital to see Dalia, Maria headed straight to her office to make a call to her detective friend who worked downtown. She wanted some background on Frank. The next day her friend called with the information she wanted. "Check's out, Maria. This guy is the real thing." Maria was satisfied with what she heard and was more comfortable having Frank on her side to help.

*   *   *   *

Maria was anxious to see Dalia. She wanted to tell her about Frank's help and she wanted to get Dalia's reaction. As soon as she saw Dalia, she knew something was wrong.

"What's wrong, sweetheart?" Maria said as she sat by her bed.

"Oh, Maria, I don't know," she was nearly in tears. She told her she was upset because Rozlin, one of Baxter's girls came up for a visit to see how she was doing. Rozlin was never a true friend of Dalia's. She was always jealous of her, and always tried to make trouble for Dalia. That's why Dalia knew that Baxter put Rozlin up to it since he wanted to know if Dalia was ready to be discharged from the hospital. "Baxter wants to know if his *property* is okay and ready to resume duties," Dalia said, with anger and sarcasm in her voice. Maria knew that Dalia provided a nice income for Baxter, she had told her this a while ago. Dalia not only turned tricks for him, but was a steady customer for his drug business. If Dalia wanted to, she could make real trouble for Baxter, and he knew it. That's why he wanted to make sure she didn't stray too far from his so-called "protection."

Maria hugged Dalia and told her not to worry. "I've already told them not to release you to anyone except me. Hey, did a fellow come up to visit you the other day?" Dalia nodded. "His name is Frank," Maria stated proudly.

"Yes, he did, and he's a little strange if you ask me. Why, do you know him?"

"Well, actually, we've talked a couple of times and believe it or not, he wants to help you."

"Help me? Help me with what?"

"After you went to the hospital, he came to see me, and wanted to know about what was going to happen to you. I told him I wasn't positive, and he expressed that he wanted to do something for you."

"What did you tell him?" asked Dalia.

"I did some checking around and I know that he's retired, his wife died a few years ago, and he's pretty wealthy. He worked for a large insurance company, and has a good pension."

"Maria, I don't know," Dalia hesitated, "I don't know if I want a stranger helping me like that. What am I going to owe him?"

"Dalia, he's not like that. Besides, the way things are going, it's not easy getting the funding to rehabilitate someone like we should, like we used to."

"Well, I'm not going to be beholden to some guy I don't know anything about."

"Dalia," Maria spoke firmly, "You may not have a choice."

"What do you mean?"

"I mean, Rozlin's probably talking to Baxter right now as we speak, and it won't be long before he'll be up here and you'll be leaving with him."

"Maria, what am I supposed to do? I can't live my life like that anymore, I'd rather be dead!" Dalia started to cry.

"Don't talk like that, child. Let's see if this Frank can do what he says he can." Maria stood up and leaned over Dalia, brushing her hair back and smoothing her forehead. "Let's give him a chance, alright? I'll give him a call and get back to you."

Maria saw the uncertainty in Dalia's eyes. "You better make up your mind, girl, you either go back to Baxter and you know what that's like, or give it a try with Frank, and see what he can do for you. See if he's good on his word. I'll be back later and you tell me your decision.

Maria rushed back to her office and gave Frank a call.

"Hello, Frank, it's Maria. Did you find an apartment yet? I'm calling because if you are going to help, like you said, you're going to have to act fast because Baxter is trying to get Dalia released to him very soon. One of his girls came up to see Dalia yesterday."

"What do you mean *very soon*?" Frank asked thoughtfully.

"Like in a day or two."

Frank paused, then answered, "No problem. I can have a place tonight if she needs it." Frank went on to explain that when his wife was sick, he added an apartment at his house attached to the garage. He set it up for a nurse to stay there because his wife needed around-the-clock care. It was a small apartment, but more than adequate, and had its own entrance separate from the main house. All Frank would have to do was have the housekeeper give it a once over and supply it fresh linens. It could be ready this evening.

"I guess you are serious about helping Dalia, aren't you, Frank? I'll go see her and let you know later today if and when she'll be coming. Thank you so much, Frank."

When Frank hung up the phone, he said, "Thank you, Laura. I know this is the right thing to do." Later that day Maria called back and told him she would bring Dalia over this evening around seven. When Maria went to the hospital, Dalia reluctantly made up her mind to have Frank help her. She knew anything was better than going back to Baxter and her life on the streets.

"Good girl, Dalia," Maria said. "I always believed in you."

*   *   *   *

The ride to Frank's place took longer than Maria expected. Frank lived in Oakdale, a suburb of the city. As they turned into the driveway to Frank's house, the setting reminded Dalia of her Aunt Jesse's place in the country, where she used to stay when she was a little girl. However, the memory didn't calm her apprehension about starting this new phase of her life. There were so many unanswered questions swirling in her head. She had no skills, sparse education, and always depended on someone else to get along. She knew that Baxter used her and even though she didn't like it, she knew what to expect form him. What did Frank want from her? Why was he helping her, a stranger? And the fact that she was so far from the city left her feeling anxious about wanting to get help if she needed it.

Frank wasn't home when Maria and Dalia reached the apartment, but they let themselves in. Maria did her best to comfort Dalia by pointing out all the *luxuries*.

A large queen size bed, her private bathroom and shower, a kitchenette where she could prepare her own meals, color TV, and a door to a patio overlooking a beautiful flower garden.

"Girl, you're living in the lap of luxury, and you're scared? I'd give up my flat in the city in a minute to live out here. What more could you ask for and what exactly are you scared of?"

"I don't know, Maria. So much has happened in the last few days. When I was a little girl and I'd go to a new foster home, I'd always felt that things were going to be better, and I'd be with my cousin Carrie again and nobody would hurt me anymore. But it never happened." Dalia said, looking down at the floor. "Things would be okay for a while, then the abuse would start all over gain, most of the time worse than what it was before. Then I'd run away, skip school, get into more trouble and all the time I just wanted things to be the way they were when I lived with Aunt Jessie and Carrie. And that's all I want now; things to be like they were then, Maria. I've been hoping for that all my life. I just wish that time could've lasted longer. Maybe all the other things wouldn't have hurt so much if the good time had lasted a little bit longer."

"Dalia," Maria took the woman's hand and said, "you can never get those times back. They're gone, you had them, you lived them, and you enjoyed them. They're gone forever. Some people never get to experience that kind of love their whole lives. You did and you miss them. It's normal to. Life is just a series of moments, some are good times, some are bad times, and most are just okay times. We live the okay times, we treasure the good times, and we do the best to eliminate the bad times. Dalia, this is the beginning of your okay times." Maria put her arms around Dalia and hugged her. Then she looked at her, placed her hand on the younger woman's chin and said, "I've got a good feeling for you, child, and things are going to be okay for you. Relax and get a good night's sleep. I promise I'll see you tomorrow."

*   *   *   *

The next morning Dalia looked out the window at the beautiful flower garden. Suddenly she heard a knock on the door. Startled, she turned from the window and saw Frank standing there with two cups of coffee on a tray. She opened the door nervously, "Can I help you?" she asked.

"I didn't know if you had time to pick up anything for breakfast this morning, but I thought you might like a cup of coffee," Frank said nervously.

"Uh, thanks, that sounds nice," Dalia said, taking a cup from Frank. They both stood awkwardly, smiling, unsure what to do next.

"Would you like to sit on the patio?" Frank asked.

"Yes, I would actually," Dalia said, slowly gaining confidence. "I was just admiring this beautiful garden."

"The garden was my wife's specialty. I just try to keep it up as best I can, but no matter if I use the same fertilizers and plant foods, they just don't come out as pretty as when Laura had it. I guess I just don't have a green thumb," he chuckled softly.

"When I lived in the country," Dalia started, "my Aunt Jessie had a huge vegetable garden. We had enough vegetables to last the winter, but she always kept a small area for her daisies and lavender. There were some gorgeous flowers that came out of that little patch." With a big smile, Dalia continued, "my Aunt Jessie used to say that vegetables provided food for the body, but flowers were food for the soul. I can see her now, bringing in a big bouquet of all kinds of petunias, hollyhocks, irises, black-eyed Suzan, and the smell would just knock you out." As her voice trailed off, Frank remembered what Maria had told him about her short stay with her aunt and cousin in the country, and how much it meant to her.

"I didn't know you lived in the country? Where exactly?" Frank asked.

"Oh, it was so long ago, sir, I was so young, I can't remember exactly the place,"

Dalia said, a bit melancholy.

Frank wasn't sure if he should go on probing. "Did you live with brothers and sisters?" he asked.

"No, just me, my Aunt Jessie, and a cousin," Dalia answered.

Frank sensed she was feeling a little uncomfortable reliving these memories, so he made an excuse and got up to leave. "Oh, before I go, would you like me to pick anything up for you? Some groceries, maybe?"

"That's very kind of you, sir, but Maria Vargas is going to stop by and we'll go shopping then. But thanks, anyway," Dalia said shyly.

*   *   *   *

The next couple of mornings Frank brought Dalia her coffee and they'd have a chat on the patio. Frank sensed that Dalia was not entirely comfortable with the arrangement, but clearly saw that she liked the apartment and definitely enjoyed the country setting. Over their morning talks, Dalia reminisced more and more about her aunt and cousin and the happy times she had in the country. Frank encouraged her to make herself at home in the garden, pick the flowers she liked and help herself to any vegetables.

Things seemed to be going okay for now, Maria thought, but knew Dalia needed some kind of training, and so far Frank had no luck finding her a job. This worried her.

*   *   *   *

At his weekly breakfast with Tom, Frank told his friend that Dalia was living in the apartment next to the garage, and that he promised her caseworker, Maria, he would find Dalia a job soon.

"Anything available at Consolidated Life?" Frank asked.

"Does she have any skills or training in the field?" Tom asked.

"I don't think so," Frank replied, shaking his head.

Sensing his pal's disappointment, Tom thought a moment, then told him how different things are today. A few years ago you could start someone in filing or the mailroom, but now even those jobs required at least some computer skills. "The only thing I can think of, Frank, is possibly a job in house-keeping or building services, but those jobs are contracted out, so I'd have to talk to the outside vendor," Tom said trying to be helpful.

Frank was not pleased with the idea, but understood the situation.

"Listen, Frank, with her background and history, and lack of skills, she's not going to be easy to place in the job market," Tom said.

"I know, buddy," Frank said downheartedly, "I just wanted to do better than a *cleaning woman* for her."

"I know, Frank, but I think it's going to be tougher than you thought it would be. Does your family know yet?"

"Not yet," Frank answered. "We're getting together tomorrow night and I'll tell them then."

"Did you tell them anything about her yet?" Tom asked.

"What do you mean, Tom?"

"You, know, do they know she's a hooker, a drug addict, a suicide victim?"

"Tom," Frank said angrily, "it's none of their business and frankly, it's none of *your* business either!" Frank pushed his plate away and started to get up from the table.

"Wait, Frank," Tom grabbed his wrist. Frank just glared at him and pulled away. "Wait, now Frank, hold on. You and your family are very close. They *should* know what you're up to. As your friend, I think it *is* my business too. Frank, I know you and I think I understand you better than a lot of people. I know what you are trying to do. I'm here to help you if I can and if you want me to. But let your family in on it. At least tell 'em, Frank." Tom sighed, "Frank, please."

"Yeah, maybe you're right."

"If they don't like it, too bad, at least you told them."

"I guess that makes the most sense, Tom. Thanks. I'll tell them tomorrow. I'll tell them everything." The two men smiled and shook hands. As they were leaving, Frank thought of something. "Hey, Tom, I know an area where you can definitely help. Dalia lived in the country a long time ago with an aunt and a cousin for about a year or so when she was very young. Her aunt was killed in a house fire and Dalia was separated form her cousin. She would like to get in touch with that cousin but has absolutely no idea how or where to start."

"I know I can help with that, Frank, but I need more information," Tom said.

"I'll find out as much as I can and get back to you. Thanks, Tom, you really are good to me." Tom smiled and patted Frank on the back.

*   *   *   *

Tom headed the records department at Consolidated Life. He was in charge of the research for lost policyholders. At Consolidated Life Insurance of America, any money paid into a policy had to be returned to the policyholder or to the beneficiaries. Many people started a policy for someone, then for one reason or another stopped paying the premiums. Consolidated Life used all resources available to locate a person that had money due them. Tom had a lot of experience locating people, and he knew if anyone could find Dalia's cousin, it would be him.

CHAPTER 5

▼

The next day Frank's family came over for their weekly dinner, family fun and games. Everyone looked forward to them. After dinner, Frank Jr., asked his Dad if he had a new housekeeper living in the garage apartment. "I thought I saw the lights on and someone inside when I drove in," he said. This was the perfect opportunity for Frank to explain to his family about Dalia and the circumstances that led up to his making the decision to help her. When Frank finished his story, there was a long pause, nobody said anything for a while. Then his oldest spoke up, "Dad, do you know what you're getting yourself into? I don't know if this is such a good idea."

"Why is that, son?" Frank asked.

"Well, Dad," Frank Jr. continued, "you don't know too much about his woman, there's a lot of valuable things in the house. Hell, she could be casing the place right now. Besides, do you think her pimp is just going to forget about her?" He shook his head back and forth, "No, I don't like the situation one bit. I don't think it's safe, you could get hurt."

"I think you're overreacting, son."

"Maybe he's right, Dad," his older daughter Carol said. "You really don't know much about her."

"Well, with the information I have from her caseworker, Ms. Vargas, I don't feel uncomfortable with her staying here," said Frank.

Then, Sharon, the youngest said, "Wait a minute, guys, I think Dad knows what he's doing. After all, he's dealt with all kinds of people throughout his whole career. I think he's a keen judge of character." Sharon went over to her father sitting at the table, and put her arms around his neck. He rubbed her forearms, "Thanks, baby," he said.

Frank explained to his children that he talked to Dalia at great length about her time with her aunt. He told them this was the only time in her life when she had any kind of break, a time when she was really happy, and then it had to end in such disaster. He told them that he thought Dalia enjoyed being in the country, and how she naturally took to gardening, even though she was with her aunt for such a short time. He also told them he wanted to help her get back on her feet and find her a job.

"Gee, Dad, what kind of jobs are available for someone with little or no training these days?" Carol asked.

"I wish I knew of something or had some connections, but at this point I haven't come up with anything, honey," he answered, and shrugged his shoulders.

As his family began to leave, Frank Jr. and Sharon stayed behind and expressed their concerns about Frank's welfare.

"Will you reconsider, Dad, or maybe make it temporary?" his son asked.

"Yeah, Dad, I agree with Frankie." Frank shook his head. "Then be careful, please, Daddy," Carol said and kissed him good-by.

Sharon was the last to say good night. "Don't worry, Dad. I think you're doing the right thing," she said as she kissed and hugged him good-by. "Hey, do you mind if I stop by to join you and your new friend for coffee some morning? I'm not that far away," she said.

"Not at all, Sharon. I'd like that."

"Thanks, Dad, good night."

"Night, honey," Frank said, as he turned off the porch light.

That night as Frank got ready for bed, he looked at Laura's picture on the nightstand, and wondered if he was doing the right thing. "Laura, I don't know what's going to happen. Am I doing the right thing? I don't know, but I feel I've got to do something. She looked so desperate that first night I saw her at the police station. Forgive me, Laura, my darling, but I realized later that the look on her face was the same look that you had after you got sick. No matter what we did, I was never able to erase that hopelessness from your face completely. And I know how we both tried, God knows how we tried. I never said anything, but I hated how that look marred your beautiful face, Laura," Frank sat down on the bed, picked up the small gilded frame. "Laura, how I wish you were here. I know you would know what to do. Good night for now, my love, and guide me to do the right thing." Frank kissed his wife's picture and fell asleep.

*   *   *   *

A few days later, Sharon stopped by to join her father and Dalia for coffee. She brought fresh pastries, and the three of them enjoyed the refreshments and the company immensely. Sharon and Dalia hit it off from the start. Sharon had many of her father's traits, and within moments Dalia felt very comfortable with Sharon as well.

"Dad, she's great," Sharon whispered in his ear when she said good bye.

Later that day, Sharon called Frank to tell him she had a client, Steve Wilcox, who owned a farm market near Oakdale, and said he was looking for some part time help to tend to his flowers and vegetables. "It would probably be just two or three days a week, Dad, until the season picks up," Sharon said.

"Great, honey, that sounds perfect."

"So, why don't you mention it to Dalia, see if she's interested, and I'd pick her up in a day or two and introduce her to Mr. Wilcox."

"Sharon, you are wonderful. I'll tell her first thing tomorrow morning."

The following morning Frank couldn't wait to tell Dalia about the job prospect. Frank thought that she'd be just as excited as he was, but was puzzled with her casual, almost bored reaction.

"Dalia," Frank said, "the shop is not that far away, and if you can't get a ride you can always walk or ride a bike." She was still less than enthusiastic and almost sullen.

"Dalia, what's the matter?" Frank asked.

"Frank, to be honest, I've never had a real job before." She went on to say she didn't believe anyone would hire her and she really didn't know much about gardening. "I just *like* flowers, that's all," she chuckled softly.

"At least talk to the owner," Frank encouraged her. "Let *him* decide if you are suitable for the job, okay?" Reluctantly, Dalia agreed and said she'd go with Sharon to meet the owner, Steve Wilcox, whenever it was convenient.

       *   *   *   *

Late that afternoon, Maria stopped by to check on Dalia. She wanted to tell her that Baxter had been around to see her, and asked about her. But before she could say anything, Dalia told her about her upcoming meeting with the owner of the farm market.

"Maria, I'm so nervous and confused, and maybe this job is not such a good idea for me right now. What do you think?" Dalia asked.

"Are you crazy, girl?" said Maria. "This is the best thing for you right now! I can understand you being nervous, but what in God's name are you confused about?"

"Maria, I can't understand why Frank and his daughter are doing this for me? Why are they helping me like this?" Dalia asked.

"What's there to understand, Dalia, except that a couple of people are doing something to help someone. Does there have to be a reason or a motive behind it, can't people just be nice or concerned about their neighbor? In the world you've been living in for most of your life, Dalia, people do things because they want something in return. The john gives you a few bucks so you'll love him. Give Baxter all your money so he'll pretend to protect you by giving you a rat infested dump to sleep in. Give me this, I'll give you that. Give me all your money, baby and I'll take care of you." Dalia looked down at her feet. She hated hearing the truth sometimes. "That's bullshit, Dalia. That's all it is … Bullshit! Look at me, Dalia. I run around all week trying to get food stamps for people, accommodations, job training, for what? … a paycheck at the end of the week? We all do things for something, girl. You know that as well as I do. And then there are the Franks of this world. They do things for other people, whether those people are family, friends, or total strangers, simply because they like people and they want people to feel good. Crazy, isn't it? No. Sometimes it's nice, just to be nice.

So, you go for that interview, get that job, all Frank wants from you is for you to take advantage of any opportunity he gives you, Dalia. Frank has done more for you in a few days than I've ever done for you. I'm right, aren't I?" Maria looked at Dalia who was still looking down, pushing the end of the rug with her feet.

"Maria, don't say that. If it weren't for you, none of this would've happened for me. You've always been the only person who ever cared for me. I'll never forget what you did for me throughout the years. And, Maria, I know you don't do what you do just for the money. You care for people, I just never realized it until now. You have always cared for me, and I don't think that I ever thanked you properly. Thank you, Maria," Dalia said as she got up and hugged Maria and started to cry on her shoulder.

"Now, now, Dalia," Maria said as she wiped the tears from Dalia's cheeks, "go get that job, live here in the country for as long as you can. From what you've been through, girl, you deserve it. This is your okay time and you make it become a good time, you remember that." Dalia smiled.

*   *   *   *

As Maria started to leave, she couldn't bring herself to tell Dalia about Baxter. She was puzzled what to do about him. The last time she talked to Baxter he was insistent on finding Dalia and her whereabouts. To Baxter, Dalia was his piece of property, a meal ticket. He had no real concern for her well being whatsoever. In his world, it was a matter of pride how many women he controlled. The only way a woman ever left a man like Baxter was when he used her up and she was of no more monetary value to him. And he let her know in no uncertain terms that she was no good to him or to anyone else. Baxter had a reputation of being ruthless and brutal when it came to controlling his women. Maria knew it was imperative that he never finds out where Dalia was living. She hoped that time would correct the situation. But no need to trouble Dalia about him just now. Dalia had too many good things going on in her life. She was thankful for that. Yet a vague uneasiness settled in her stomach that she didn't like, but was likely to ignore for the moment.

*   *   *   *

The day Sharon picked up Dalia to meet Steve Wilcox, Dalia was a nervous wreck. She was concerned about how she looked, what she wore, and what she should say.

"Just relax and be yourself," Sharon told her.

"Be myself?" said Dalia, "but who am I? A few short weeks ago I was a hooker and a drug addict on the streets, just trying to survive. I couldn't do anything without Baxter's permission and according to him, everything I did was wrong. No matter what I ate, what I wore, where I bought my clothes, nothing was ever right. What makes me think I'm going to do all right now?" Sharon didn't know what to say. She looked at Dalia, and saw in her eyes what her father saw. Sharon hugged Dalia and said,

"You'll be all right, don't worry."

As Sharon and Dalia drove out, Frank saw them and motioned for them to stop.

"I just wanted to say how nice you both look," Frank said, as he reached in the car window to shake hands with Dalia, and wish her luck. He saw that she was nervous and said, "You'll be okay."

"Thank you, Frank," Dalia said, and smiled to herself as they drove off.

*   *   *   *

As they drove up to the Wilcox Farm, the smell of freshly turned soil brought a smile to Dalia's face. The memories of her Aunt Jessie and Carrie came flooding back to her, and she knew that she wanted to work at the farm very much. But, then she started to worry again about whether or not she'd say the right thing or if she looked okay. Her heart pounded when she saw a man drive up in a pick-up truck.

Steve Wilcox had been farming for about three years now. As a young man he worked at several farms during his summer vacations from high school and college. After he earned his degree, he worked as a manufacturer's representative and was very successful. But he always loved farming, and after ten years of working in the corporate world, he decided to buy an abandoned farm and strike out on his own. Even though the last three years were tough, through his hard work and dedication to quality, his farm market paid off.

The interview with Steve wasn't much of an interview at all. While Steve unloaded some plants from his truck, he told Dalia what her duties would be.

"Dalia, you'll be helping me out with whatever has to be done. One day it could be weeding, another watering or planting, whatever. If you think you can handle it, you can start tomorrow afternoon," he said, wiping his gloved hands on his jeans. She just looked at him, thinking how easy it was. Dalia could hardly contain herself as she thanked Steve and assured him she'd be there tomorrow whenever he wanted her.

The ride back to the apartment was nothing like the ride to the farm market. Dalia was as giddy as a schoolgirl with her first crush. She told Sharon how hard she was going to work and that she'd do her best to help Steve's business any way she could. Sharon couldn't help but smile and feel good for Dalia. This was the happiest Dalia had been in years. Her father was partly responsible for that, and she felt warmth in her stomach about how she was proud of him.

*   *   *   *

It wasn't hard to see the change in Dalia after she started her job at the farm. Because of her schedule, Frank and Dalia didn't have coffee as often on the patio. And when they did, she talked more and more about her time with Aunt Jessie and her cousin Carrie. She told him that working on the farm reminded her of her aunt's farm because people would stop and buy vegetables from her aunt. Dalia elaborated on the kinds of vegetables Aunt Jessie grew in the garden and the different customers that she'd sell to. There was always the widower who asked Aunt Jessie for her recipes or the young newlywed who didn't know the first thing about cooking. Dalia loved her Aunt Jessie and felt a void in her life without her ever since.

One morning over breakfast, Frank asked Dalia what her aunt's last name was.

"I never knew it," Dalia said, "she was always just Aunt Jessie. But there was an old man that used to come by to help my aunt once in a while and Auntie would feed him whenever he stopped working. My cousin and I would laugh and laugh whenever he said 'thank you, Miss Whiskers, thank you, Miss Whiskers' because he had a funny lisp, but that's all I remember about her name."

"Would you like to try to find your cousin Carrie and visit her?" Frank asked.

"Oh, yes, I would, very much so, but I wouldn't know where to start," Dalia said "I have a friend whose job is to locate people. He works for the company I used to work for and if anyone can find her, I think he can."

"Frank," Dalia said softly, "that would be so nice, but I don't know."

"Don't know what, Dalia? You don't know if you'd like to see her or talk to Carrie, just to see if she's okay?" Frank was puzzled. He thought this is what would make her happy.

"It's not that, Frank. I don't know, you know, what would she think?"

"Think about what? Dalia, you don't know what kind of life she's had either. Maybe she needs you, did you ever think of that?"

"No," Dalia said softly.

"If you two had so much fun together and all these great memories, why don't you at least give it a try, find out what she's up to." Dalia was silent. "C'mon, Dalia, why don't you meet my friend Tom, he'll know what questions to ask to jog your memory. It will take him a couple of weeks to work on it, so you have plenty of time to decide about whether or not you want to contact Carrie."

"All right," Dalia said, smiling.

*   *   *   *

A meeting with Tom was arranged and the three of them met over dinner the following week. After some small talk, Tom asked Dalia the specifics about her life in the country with her relatives. He asked about school, the weather, shops and stores, church, and the post office. What kind of people, the ethnic and racial make up of townspeople, ages, social status. Tom asked every possible question drawing a composite of the community in his head. Tom's interrogation jogged Dalia's memory, even surprising herself, how much she remembered. Before long Dalia was recalling things without Tom's prompting.

From the meeting, Tom estimated that Dalia lived with her aunt for about a year and a half. He gathered that the town was near a lake, since Dalia remembered she and Carrie would often go swimming on hot days and have so much fun playing in the sand and building sandcastles. It was also a valuable piece of information since it narrowed down where he could start looking. Tom also questioned Maria Vargas, and with her additional information he told Frank and Dalia, he'd see what he could do and get back to them in a few days. Tom loved a challenged and he liked the fact he was helping Frank.

CHAPTER 6

▼

Tom was anxious to get started on the investigation, although, it presented more of a challenge than the mundane kind of work he normally did. Tom was looking for a rural community in the surrounding area that was racially mixed prior to the integration efforts of the sixties and seventies, either in this county or the outer counties on Majestic Lake. Majestic Lake was of the shallowest of the seven surrounding lakes in the region, and people loved it because of the wealth of trout fishing and the quiet, non commercial setting. From the information he got from Dalia, Tom believed that the area was no more than a couple of hours from the city.

Because of the proximity to the Canadian border, there were several nearby communities active during the abolitionist movement of the 1800's and therefore, it was not uncommon for these rural areas to have up to three or four generations of African American families.

Tom concentrated his efforts on these areas and started his search by looking at newspaper accounts for a house fire in the 1960s that took the life of an elderly woman. After exhausting almost all the towns and villages on his list, he came across an article about a Mrs. Whittakers who died in a fire on January 10, 1969, in the town of Marley, about sixty miles from Rochester. Tom made a few phone calls, and after speaking to the secretary from Marley Central School and a woman from the newspaper, he decided to drive up there himself and see if he could find out first hand about the goings on in Marley.

While he prepared for his trip he remembered what Dalia had said about "Mrs. Whiskers" and he suddenly realized he must be on the right track. "Mrs. Whiskers sounds like Whittakers," he shouted out loud, "That's got to be it." Tom was overjoyed, he solved the first part of the clue to unlocking Dalia's past. He wanted to call Frank, but thought better if he waited. He wanted to have the whole story to present to his friend.

*   *   *   *

Marley was a community back in the 1800's whose citizens were concerned about the effect that slavery was having on the whole country. Many people in the area were active in hiding and supplying papers for the runaway slaves who were trying to make it to Canada. Marley was one of the major stops for the systems of hideaways that became known as the "under ground railroad" After the civil war, many African Americans families settled in Marley and the surrounding towns.

James Whittakers had heard about Marley and came north during the Great Depression of the 1930's. He promised his young wife Jesse that as soon as he had a decent job and a house he would send for her. James was a hard worker and an excellent farmer but he knew he never got a fair cut from the land he was sharecropping. He felt he would have more opportunity in the north.

Soon after he arrived he found work at a large farm outside of Marley. Ruben Gault who was a better businessman than he was a farmer owned almost a thousand acres of fertile soil and would plant the crop that would bring him the most money even though planting the same thing year after year would exhaust the land. There were years that he would have to leave large tracts unplanted because his yields were so small.

After James worked for Ruben a couple of years, Ruben began to listen to this young black farmer who had an innate ability to produce larger and better yields. James explained to Ruben that crops were like people, you had to mix and match the different crops so that they would work together and complement each other. Within the same field James would plant rows of corn, wheat and other crops. James said that each plant or crop had certain strengths and weaknesses that they would share with the other plants so that when combined they flourished.

By taking James Whittakers' advice Ruben Gault's farm prospered and he became one of the largest produce distributors in the state.

Ruben appreciated what James had done for him and over the protests of his three sons, rewarded his loyal and gifted farm hand by giving him a 50-acre tract of land in the town of Marley. Now James Whittakers would be able to send for his beloved Jesse. By the time Jesse arrived James had built a sturdy cabin on his land in Marley and even though he continued to work for Ruben he was hard at work planting a variety of fruits and vegetables that he could sell at the local markets. Jesse worked right along with her husband planting, weeding and cultivating. James taught Jesse his method of mixing and matching crops until she too was as proficient a farmer as James was.

James and Jesse were unable to have children so after a few years they began to take in foster children. Over the years there were times when there would be up to ten or twelve children living in their home at one time. James and Jesse not only provided a place for these children to live but they made sure that each and every one of them got a good education and at least graduated from high school. Many of their foster children went on to become teachers, nurses, lawyers and engineers, farmers and all kinds of tradesmen, James and Jesse always taught their children that if they treated each other and the people around them with respect then they would always be respected and treated like ladies and gentlemen.

What a sight it was to see James and Jesse and their flock of children going to Sunday services. All the girls were dressed in their finest dresses and the boys in their Sunday suits.

After Ruben Gault died, James was able to concentrate on building up his own farm business. He was so successful that he was able to purchase more land and equipment, making him one of the most prominent farmers in the entire county. The home he built for his family was one of the largest and finest in Marley.

*   *   *   *

Tom arrived in Marley early Friday morning and decided to go to the elementary school first. The school was fairly new, he thought, but still hopeful he would get some information. He knew student records were kept for twenty years or better. The woman behind the first desk told him records from the 1960s were available at the county seat about twenty-five miles south of Marley. "That's procedure," she kept repeating after every question he asked.

"Are there any teachers still around from that era?" Tom asked the woman, hoping she'd be more helpful.

"Mrs. Dexter, the principal, used to teach second grade. Maybe she can help you, the woman said. "Good luck with that one," she said not looking at him, banging away on her keyboard.

Mrs. Dexter was a small woman in her early sixties who appeared "all business," but her greeting was as warm as her smile was pleasant. Tom assured her that he wouldn't take much of her time.

"Don't be silly, sir, I'm glad to be of any help I can," Mrs. Dexter said. "Please have a seat," indicating to the chair in front of him.

"Thank you, kindly," he started as he sat down. "I'm from Consolidated Life, and am doing some investigating about a house fire that killed a Mrs. Whittakers around 1969."

"Yes, indeed," Mrs. Dexter said without hesitation, "that fire devastated the whole community. Mrs. Whittakers was well known and respected by everyone in Marley and even the surrounding counties. She raised the finest flowers and vegetables in the county, prize winning, they were. People would come from all over just to buy her produce. I don't think there's been a larger funeral in these parts in the last forty years."

"Is that right?" Tom said, his hand cupping his chin. "Did you know anything about what happen to the girls she was caring for, Mrs. Dexter?

"Not really, unfortunately. She loved those girls too," she said sadly, shaking her head.

"Do you remember the girls at all?" Tom continued, hoping to jog her memory like he did Dalia's.

"Well, one did have a kind of odd name, at least odd for those days, if you know what I mean."

"Dalia?" Tom said questioningly.

"Yes, Dalia, that's what it was, Dalia, and what a pretty little girl she was, such beautiful eyes … and the other one?" Mrs. Dexter inquired.

"Carrie," said Tom.

"Of course," said Mrs. Dexter. "Carrie and Dalia, those girls were inseparable, like two peas in a pod. Always dressed just so, nice and perfect, not so much as a hair ribbon out of place. They were perfect little ladies. Naturally, from what I was told, only ladies and gentleman came from Mrs. Whittakers."

"Did Mrs. Whittakers have other children?" Tom asked.

"No, not at that time, she was getting on in years by then. I believe years ago she used to take foster children on a regular basis when her husband was still alive. Then that terrible fire," she sighed, looking at Tom, then down at her hands, then up, as if in silent prayer to the heavens.

"Did the girls continue to come to school after the fire?" Tom asked.

"No," Mrs. Dexter said, shaking her head slowly. "A crying shame, a real crying shame."

"Would there be anyone who might remember Mrs. Whittakers and the girls personally, Mrs. Dexter?" Tom didn't want to appear disrespectful, but his questions were necessary for him to be successful.

"I'm not sure, but there was a Mrs. Williams who used to be Mrs. Whittakers closest neighbor on Route 40. Just take Main Street to Baker's Corners, and the first right is Route 40. Go for about five miles and you'll see a house with lots of birdfeeders, that Mrs. Williams, she loves her birds."

"Thank you for all your help, Mrs. Dexter," Tom said as they shook hands and he nearly ran to his car. Tom was pleased with the information so far and was anxious to meet this Mrs. Williams.

*   *   *   *

Just outside of town off the main road, like Mrs. Dexter said, was a cluster of four or five neat box like houses. One of these was where Mrs.Williams lived, the one with a cluster of trees and plenty of birdfeeders.

"Hello," Tom said politely to the tall young woman who answered the door.

"Can I help you?" she said.

"Yes, I'm looking for a Mrs. Williams."

"She's my aunt, I'm her niece Dawn. What can she do for you?" Just then Clara Williams stepped into the room after she heard Tom's voice, and piqued her interest when she heard him mention the name "Dalia." Clara Williams was a robust woman, whose speech and appearance defied her eighty-five years.

The older woman asked their guest to come in, and had Dawn prepare tea, while she and Tom sat in the living room.

"How are Dalia and Carrie?" Clara Williams asked.

"Actually, Dalia is okay, but the reason I'm here is to find out about Carrie.

Do you know her whereabouts?"

"You know, sir, I always worried about those girls. It was a shame how they were separated."

"Did you know the details of their circumstances after the fire?" Tom asked. "After Jesse Whittakers died?"

"Yes, I do, they lived here in this house when the people from the agencies came to get the girls. You see, we didn't know what to do with them after the fire. We didn't even know if they had family or anything. Those poor girls were so scared. They must have come from tough backgrounds, because they seemed to blossom with their Aunt Jesse. They were so happy and felt secure with that woman, bless her soul," Clara added.

"Unfortunately, more than one person was concerned for the girls, and that's why two different social workers came to take care of them. And would you believe they showed up on the same day?" Dawn came in with a tray of tea and biscuits. Clara nodded to her niece, and in turn the girl poured two cups of tea and placed them on the coffee table bedside her aunt. She looked at Tom and smiled, as her aunt continued with her story.

"The girls were playing in the next room, right there," she pointed to a small den, "when the county social services lady came to get the girls. Within five minutes, can you believe, a sister from the orphanage came to pick up the girls too. The weather was terrible that day, I remember a bad snowstorm. Both women drove all this way out in the bad weather and I guess they didn't want a wasted trip. They were determined," she said raising her eyebrows while taking a sip of tea. "Hmmm," Tom said, nodding with the woman.

"Then there was a question as to which agency should take the poor things. So both women called their offices, until a decision was made. After several phone calls back and forth, it was determined that each agency would take one girl. I tried to tell them the girls shouldn't be separated, but it didn't seem to matter to them. To make matters worse, both agencies had to agree who would take which child. The Rev. Paul Sadler, pastor of our local church, settled the matter by flipping a coin. Can you believe that?" Clara shook her head. Tom nodded while biscuit crumbs fell around his mouth. "Dalia went with the county lady, and Carrie with the Sister. The girls had to be forcibly separated so that the people could get on their ways. It was a sad day, and a shame the way those girls were pulled apart, literally, they hugged and cried until the very end."

"What a shame," Tom agreed.

"Now, tell me please, about that Dalia, and those beautiful eyes?" She smiled. "Do her eyes still speak for her? You know, you could always tell how that girl felt just by looking at her eyes. Joy, hurt, anger, or contentment. When she first came to Jesse's there was a lot of hurt and anger in those eyes. But after a while, it turned to joy, and happiness, and love. Yes, a lot of love, and it radiated her whole face."

"Do you know anything about the lady who brought Dalia to Aunt Jesse's?

"No, I don't, but she must've had a good case for Dalia, because even though Jesse used to take foster children when she was younger, she wasn't taking any at that time. Carrie had only been with Jesse for a week or so, and I do believe she was a distant relative of one of Jesse's former foster children. Later, Jesse told me that she was glad that she had taken Dalia, because the two girls got along famously, like they were sisters." She took another sip of tea, wiped her mouth with a napkin and turned to Tom. "Now let me shut up, and you tell me about my girl Dalia."

"Well, after a rough time in the big city, a few bumps and bruises, she's living in a nice apartment and working at a farm market," sparing the details for Clara's sake.

"What a shame, I was worried about her getting involved with city life," Clara shook her head.

"She's happy now, Mrs. Williams, you can rest at ease on that. She's met some good people."

"I'd like to see her," Clara said.

"She'd like to see you too," Tom answered.

"And if you find out anything about Carrie, please let me know."

"Of course, Mrs. Williams," Tom said, as he got up and started to head toward the door. "Thank you for everything, the hospitality, and the information." Tom felt a sense of relief from Mrs. Williams, and while he drove back to town, knew he was close to finding Carrie.

*   *   *   *

Tom realized his objective was to find where Carrie lived now. However, he couldn't figure out who was the mysterious Mrs. Robinson, who showed up in Maria Vargas' file, as the person who took Dalia to Jesse Whittakers' home. He was confident that he would find Carrie by checking records of Catholic orphanages in 1969 or 1970. That would be his next step. He gave Frank a call when he got back and told him what he'd discovered so far. Both men found it incredible how the two girls were separated, and how a flip of a coin would determine the fate of each of them.

*   *   *   *

Tom found assessing the records at the orphanages was not as easy as he thought. Because of privacy laws, most of the records were sealed. After he filed for a petition and explained the circumstances of his search, Mr. Rathbone, the director of the Catholic orphanages in the region, agreed to contact the individual to see if she wanted to get in touch with Tom and

Dalia. "The person in question," Mr. Rathbone insisted, "must be given the courtesy and respect first. This is the way it has always been done."

"Yes, of course," Tom agreed.

"This may take a few days or even weeks, you understand," Mr. Rathbone said.

"However long it takes," Tom assured him, "I will wait." The two men parted politely, and Mr. Rathbone agreed to call Tom when he had some information.

*   *   *   *

Meanwhile, Tom turned his attention to finding Mrs. Robinson. In the late 1950s the city built apartments known as the Hallover Homes. These were meant to be "modern" living to inner city residents. Because of poor design, substandard materials, and the city's lack of mandating proper maintenance, the "projects" as they became better known as, were a breeding ground for crime, abuse, and discontent. This was the environment Dalia Preston was born into. In the 1990s, the city deemed the Hallover Homes unacceptable for living, so they were razed and replaced with modern duplexes called "Ranchford Knolls." Many of the families who had to leave the Hallover Homes moved into the Ranchford Knolls neighborhood. This is where Tom started his search for Mrs. Robinson, on the suggestion of Maria Vargas.

After he checked family names from all the Hallover Homes against the present names from Ranchford Knolls, Tom came up with several matches. After a few interviews,

Tom met with Rosetta Witherspoon, a woman in her late seventies, who lived in the same building as the Prestons in the 1960s. She was there when Dalia was born. According to Rosetta, Casey Preston, Dalia's mother, went into severe labor all of a sudden, and it was too late to get her to a hospital. Rosetta, a registered nurse, lived on the floor below, and was called by the neighbors to help. "She was in such intense pain and scared to death," Rosetta recalled to Tom when they finally met for a coffee one day, "and I didn't think she was going to make it. It was a difficult birth because the baby was not turned properly in the birth canal, and the cord was wrapped around the baby's neck. We all thought that baby would be strangled. After several tense and anxious moments," Rosetta continued, "I was able to get the baby turned around, and she was born. That cord was wrapped so tight around her neck, it's a wonder she didn't come out dead. My, oh, my!" exclaimed Rosetta.

"After she was out, it took a heck of long time and some frantic moves on my part to get that child breathing on her own, it did." Tom was amazed at what he heard. Rosetta went on to explain that she had taken an interest in African culture and even studied African languages and dialects. She remembered a phrase in one of her culture books that meant "superior strength," "determination," "strong will to survive and flourish," among other noble attributes. The phrase was "D'ha lal liah." After the near tragic birth of this beautiful baby, Rosetta couldn't help but whisper the phrase over and over as she held this newborn infant in her arms, close to her little ears. When she told the other women in the room what the words meant, they all started calling the baby "Dalia," and that's how she got her name.

"After Dalia's birth, I became very close to Casey Preston. Casey loved that baby girl. She wanted only the best for her. She was determined to finish high school, get a decent job, and make a good home for her and her baby Dalia. As Dalia grew up and learned how to talk, her mother confided in me and would say how proud her father would've been of his daughter. But she never told anyone who Dalia's father was.... .but I always had a feeling I knew who he was already." She looked at Tom, boastful that she had a secret.

"Would you mind telling me?" Tom asked. The woman shook her head. She refused because she wasn't one hundred percent sure and didn't want to start rumors at this stage.

"Do you know a Mrs. Robinson?" Tom asked.

"What do you know about her?" Rosetta asked.

"Nothing, really," Tom replied, confused by Rosetta's defensive like behavior.

"She's mentioned in Dalia's files as the woman who took Dalia to live with Jesse Whittakers in Marley. That's all I have to go on," he said.

"What are you talking about?" Rosetta asked.

At this point Tom explained everything to Rosetta about Dalia and why he was asking for information.

"Casey Preston was killed," Rosetta said. "Then the girl went into foster care and I lost track of her. But I always wondered what happened to her and if her father had ever come around."

"That's why I would like to know who the father is," Tom suggested again. Again Rosetta refused, but told him,

"Why don't you ask Mrs. Robinson?"

"Do you know where she lives?" asked Tom.

"Not anymore, but they used to live in the projects at the same time the Prestons did. They had a son who was a little older than Casey, and he was sweet on her."

"What happened to them?"

"Oh, it's quite a long story, sir. Back then if you remember, there was quite a bit of turmoil not only in this city, but the whole country. Conditions in the cities were terrible. The inner city schools were run down, you couldn't find decent housing or jobs. If a black man or woman had a job, any job, the opportunity for advancement was non-existent. There was prejudice everywhere. There was rioting and even our city was feeling the effects of this turmoil."

"So when Mr. Robinson was promoted at the utility company, and was able to move to an all white neighborhood, it was quite the talk you can imagine. There were those who were genuinely glad for the family, and then on the other hand, there were those who were extremely jealous. Back then if you had a chance to get out of the projects, you did. And then more often than not, you almost had to distance yourself from the old neighborhood. That's just the way it was back then." Rosetta looked somber, she closed her eyes and sighed heavily.

"Did the Robinsons come around after Casey was killed?" Tom asked.

"Their son came around a few times before Dalia was born, but that was it as far as I could remember. Mrs. Robinson came by once after Casey died and asked about Dalia. She seemed to be upset when she was told social services had taken her away."

"Rosetta, do you think that the Robinson boy is Dalia's father?" Tom asked tentatively.

"Mr. Dutton," Rosetta said firmly, "you found me, why don't you find Mrs. Robinson." The woman got up slowly, extended her hand and saw Tom to the door. As he started to walk away, she called over to him, "Sir, wait, one last thing, does Dalia still have those beautiful eyes?"

"Yes, she does Mam." Rosetta smiled.

"Please say hello to her for me, and tell her I always knew she'd be okay because she's 'D' ha lal liah!'"

CHAPTER 7

▼

Tom could hardly wait for the next day to contact City Electric & Gas Company to find out about Mr. Robinson and where he lived now. Tom estimated that the Robinsons were probably in their late sixties or early seventies, so he figured that they must be retired at this time. First thing in the morning Tom contacted the human resource department of City Electric and found there were about four men with the name Robinson who had retired. So Tom had to pay each one a visit.

By the second house, a place in the suburb of the city, Tom knew he had the right one. The door was answered by a tall woman, casually dressed in plaid slacks and red sweater, and wore a pleasant smile.

"Good day mam, my name is Tom Dutton, I'm looking for information about families who used to live in the Hallover Homes back in the late 1950's and 60s."

"Well, Mr. Dutton, it was so long ago. I don't know if I can be of any help to you. Would you like to come in?" the woman offered. While she lead Tom into the hallway, a tall, distinguished looking man appeared from the next room. A grin crept across his face and he softly said, "Oh, boy, that sure was a long time ago."

"Indeed it was, sir," Tom said, as he offered the man his hand.

"Mr. Robinson," the man said.

"Reggie," his wife called to him, "have a seat. This nice gentleman wants to know something about the old neighborhood." She offered Tom a seat, then sat across from him, while Reggie continued to stand. "Well, Mr. Dutton, what would you like to know exactly about Hallover Homes?" She smiled as she crossed her fingers and put them in her lap.

"Specifically," Tom said, "do you know a Dalia Preston?"

Suddenly, Mrs.Robinson lost her smile and became nervous. She uncrossed her legs and hands. She dropped her head and started to fidget at the hem of her sweater. She looked sad and confused. Mr. Robinson left the room abruptly.

"Who sent you here, Mr. Dutton?" she said finally.

"No one sent me, I'm here on behalf of Dalia. She's trying to connect to her past."

"That was a long time ago, Mr. Dutton. And frankly, I don't know what to say."

Before Tom had a chance to speak, Mr. Robinson called his wife from the other room. "Excuse me, Mr. Dutton," she said apologetically.

Mrs. Robinson returned a few minutes later and told Tom that she suddenly remembered an appointment and that he best leave. "I'm awfully sorry, Mr. Dutton," she said, "but you do understand?"

"Can you tell me anything?" he asked earnestly.

"I'm sorry, sir, I really have to get ready for my appointment. Please excuse me." As she led him to the door, Tom thought he'd ask one more time.

"Mrs. Robinson, this is very important. I've come this far, can't you please help me?" She looked at him as if she wanted to say something, but couldn't. Her eyes searched his face, then looked away. "Here's my card. I'll appreciate it if you contact me."

"I'll see. I can't promise. Good-bye, Mr. Dutton," she said, as she closed the door.

Tom walked away bewildered. He unnerved them, and had to rely on Mrs. Robinson having a change of heart.

When Dorothy came back into the house, she could see her husband sitting on the sofa reading the morning newspaper as if nothing had happened. After a few moments of silence, he commented on the current state of affairs in politics and made an off-hand remark.

"Reggie," his wife said curtly, "How can you just sit there and act as if Mr. Dutton was never here?"

"What do you want me to say, Dorothy?" He put the paper down. "That is none of our business, we've been through this before. What do they want from me now?"

"Reggie, after thirty years what could she possibly want from you? Except maybe to find out about her grandfather and grandmother who could have been there if she needed them?" Dorothy said wistfully, her hands shaking by her side.

"Don't say that, Dorothy, you don't know that. How can you know that, woman?"

"Reggie, I know it and for God's sake you know it too!" she cried angrily. "You just never wanted to admit to it, that our son fell in love with his childhood sweetheart, a girl from the ghetto, and that love produced a beautiful little girl that we ignored all these years. Our own flesh and blood, Reggie, if you only knew," her voice trailed off, tears falling down her cheeks.

"Knew *what*, Dorothy? What did I not know?"

"Oh, Reggie, there are some things I never told you."

"What things, Dorothy?" Reggie said calmly, a slow anger building in his voice.

"Things about Bill, Casey Preston, and the baby." Dorothy, hesitated at first, then sat down and finally told her husband what she had done so many years ago. She told him everything, the visits to Casey in the old neighborhood after they had moved, about being concerned for Dalia's welfare, and finally taking her to Jessie Whittakers in Marley, where she knew she'd be safe. She told him about a letter their son wrote about wanting to make a home for his daughter. Finally, the whole story was out, and what a relief.

"Tomorrow, Reggie, yes, tomorrow, I'm calling Mr. Dutton. It's probably too late, but I'd like to see my granddaughter, if she wants to see me." Reggie sat, unable to move or speak or even react. Dorothy had blind sided him, took him completely off guard. After a few minutes, without a word, he went back to his paper.

*   *   *   *

Tom couldn't wait to tell Frank what he'd uncovered so far, especially what happened at the Robinson's. He knew his friend would be pleased. He considered Dalia, too, and was anxious to see what she thought of the news.

*   *   *   *

Because of her schedule, Frank and Dalia couldn't meet on the patio in the mornings for coffee as often as they used to. Instead, quite often they shared a few minutes by the garden, talking and sharing friendly conversation. Frank enjoyed these casual meetings, when Dalia would report what she did at the farm market that particular day, who came in, who bought what, and so on… At times it reminded him of how Laura was when she first started her business and how excited she would get telling him about the events of the day, the small mishaps and quiet successes. It always pleased him how rewarding it was for her. Like with Laura, Frank sensed a similar transformation in Dalia, and was amazed at how confident and sure of herself she was becoming. She was talking more and more, and sharing stories about her time in the country with Aunt Jessie. She even looked forward to telling Carrie about her work now, and anticipated their reunion. It was like her life on the street and her association with Baxter never happened.

Dalia couldn't believe how genuinely interested Frank was in her work at Steve Wilcox's farm. She was amazed at how attentive and patient he was in what she was doing. No man had ever shown her or expressed an interest like he did, for anything except for the sex she provided or for how much money she could make for him. Up until she met Frank, all the men she ever knew were interested in how they could use her for their own good. If she ever expressed an opinion or did so much as disagree with something they said or did, she was quickly put in her place by deprivation or a beating.

The severity of the beating was not according to the so-called infraction, but the whim of Baxter. The most humiliating beatings were those that were done in front of his friends, just so he could "show off."

Dalia had never known a man like Frank. She still couldn't understand why he would do all this for her. The apartment, the job, the friendship, and all for nothing in return, she thought, how could she be so lucky? Sometimes she would lie awake at night and think how her life had changed so much since she met Frank, and she would feel confused. She almost didn't know how to act. He was so kind and funny in a charming way, that sometimes she found herself daydreaming about him. He made her feel almost like a schoolgirl. She'd think how happy she was, happier than she had been in years, since she last lived on the farm with Carrie and Aunt Jessie. She would wonder if this was really happening to her. It seemed a dream, one she never wanted to wake up from. Knowing the whole time she owed this all to Frank. How would she ever repay him? Did she have to? Did he expect it? These questions plagued her at night, made her dizzy and restless, until she was fast asleep.

*   *   *   *

It was only a few days before Mrs. Robinson contacted Tom. They arranged to meet at a restaurant. Tom was more anxious to hear her story than she was to tell it. Dorothy Robinson was very nervous when she arrived, and before she would begin talking, she had to know how Dalia was.

"She's okay now," Tom said, "but she has had some difficult times. Dalia made her living on the streets as a prostitute. She has battled drug addiction and attempted suicide at least once since I've known her." Tom sensed this was very painful for Dorothy to hear, and felt sorry for her. However, he didn't mince words when he came straight to the point, "Are you related to her, Mrs. Robinson?"

"She's my granddaughter," the woman answered and started to cry. Tom had a feeling she was, but it still came as a shock when he heard the words, and was confused.

"What happened? I can't seem to put the pieces together," he said.

"Mr. Dutton…. do you mind if I call you Tom?" Mrs. Robinson asked. Tom nodded. She took a drink from a tall-stemmed water glass, wiped her lips and told her story. "I always hoped for the best with that girl, but in the back of my mind, I was afraid for the worst."

"Aren't you the person who took Dalia to her Aunt Jesse's in Marley? And why didn't you take her after the fire?"

"I didn't know about the fire and I couldn't take her anyway," she said regretfully.

"You couldn't or you didn't want to?" Tom could tell that Mrs. Robinson resented that last remark.

"Tom, you didn't know those times and you'll never understand them. You will never know what it's like to wear my skin, do you?" she said sharply.

"Try me," he challenged her. "Tell me what happened. Tell me why you didn't take your granddaughter after the fire at Aunt Jesse's?" Dorothy looked uncomfortable, he nearly thought she might leave. He softened his tone, and coaxed her to talk about it

Dorothy looked up.

"My husband worked for the City Electric & Gas Company for many years. He was a good worker, loyal and trustworthy, and even had some college under his belt, but in those days blacks weren't promoted. There were no exceptions. Well, if you remember, back in 1967 there was a riot in our city. It was a wake up call for a lot of people. After all those years, folks realized that maybe things weren't right in the black communities. The city leaders got after the big companies in town and wanted to know why there were so few blacks on their payrolls and no blacks in management. It was just plain unfair, if you ask me. It caused quite a stink in this fine town of ours, where everyone thought things were okay.

Well things weren't okay and my husband happened to be in the right place at the right time. Reggie didn't agree with the rioters or their methods, but he benefited from their actions. Soon after the dust settled, Reggie was called down to corporate headquarters and was offered a position in management. A few days later he was told if he wanted to move to a nicer neighborhood … in those days 'nicer' meant 'whiter' … the Company would help him get a mortgage. This is what Reggie had wanted for so long, and nothing was going to stand in his way. Nothing! Do you hear me, Tom, this man was finally going to get all the advantages he and his family deserved." Mrs. Robinson wiped the sweat that was forming on her forehead. She took another long drink of water.

"Can I get you anything, Mrs. Robinson," Tom asked, he was intrigued and wanted to hear more.

"No Tom, I just want you to listen carefully, so the facts are clear. Soon we moved, but my son, Bill, would go back to see Casey Preston every chance he'd got. He was no more than a boy, you understand, but he had his head and heart set on Casey, and he had to do this, mind you, behind his father's back. He was so much in love with that girl. Well, guess what, Tom, the age-old story, boy meets girl, boy loves girl, boy gets girl pregnant. It couldn't have happened at a worse time as far as Reggie was concerned. The new job, the new neighbor-hood, a lot was going on in our lives. And, I repeat, nothing was going to stand in the way of Bill's education, going to col-lege and getting the degree that his father never got. My hus-band forbade all of us from going back to that neighborhood for anything. I had never known him to be like that, and it was probably the most trying and heartbreaking times for our family. I swore it was going to tear us part. I was torn between appeasing my husband and protecting my son.

After the baby was born, I tried to keep track of Casey and Dalia as much as I could without Reggie finding out, but it was increasingly difficult to sneak about visiting and making phone calls. Even though I couldn't be a part of Dalia's life, I was satisfied that Casey was doing a fine job raising her daughter. She loved that child so much, and she was a good mother...."

"What about your son?" Tom interrupted.

"Bill was broken hearted of course, torn between doing the responsible thing for his child and obeying his father's wishes. He started college, and I don't really know for sure but I think he stayed in contact with Casey. We never really mentioned it after a while. I didn't like it, at first, but up until Casey was hit by a car, I was okay with the situation. I accepted it, like I've done my whole life with unsatisfactory conditions. But after the accident and I found out Dalia was put into foster care, I was very upset, guilty in a way, I felt my hands were tied. Even though I tried to keep track of her, I knew she was placed in several different homes and I knew that was suspect. I feared for her welfare. Through a friend, I heard about Jesse Whittakers in Marley, and I made the trip one day to see if she would take Dalia. I thought the change of scenery, would be good for a child growing up. I was disappointed when Jesse was reluctant to help. But when I explained my fears for Dalia's welfare, Jesse finally agreed. I promised her I would send money every month, but Jesse would have no part of that. 'I never take children for money,' she said to me, she took them in because they needed her, and never wanted any of her children to ever think her love was paid for. The day I brought Dalia up there was one of the worst days of my life. Dalia was beginning to be scarred from the many foster homes she was living at. She was such a beautiful child, what beautiful eyes she had, soulful and kind, but scared and pitiful too. It broke my heart to leave her there. The only thing that made me go through with it was that I knew she was going to be happy and safe with Jesse. Jesse would provide the love and affection she needed, the luxuries of being a child and freedom from the tension of the city. But you remember, Tom, all this was behind my husband's back, I couldn't share it with anybody. I felt so unfaithful."

"How about after the fire then, Dorothy?"

"Tom, you have to understand, I put total trust in Jesse to look after Dalia, and I didn't pay that much attention to what was happening in Marley. And with Reggie's attitude, I had to keep myself busy and attentive to our own affairs, by that time other things took front and center in our lives. Bill was in college by then, he enrolled in ROTC, and after he graduated he got his commission and joined the army as a second lieutenant. He had less than a month to go on his tour of duty in Vietnam, when a sniper killed him in DaNang. It was a long while before I even wanted to think about Dalia. "Oh, Tom," Dorothy sniffed and wiped the corners of her eyes wet with fresh tears. "It was a terrible time for us, I thought Reggie would die from the heartbreak, our only son, our baby. He put all his hopes and dreams on Bill, like any father would do."

"I'm so sorry, Dorothy," Tom said. He gently squeezed her hand across the table.

"Tom, I have a letter I always carry in my pocketbook, I want you to see. It's from Bill. His father has never seen it." Dorothy handed the letter to Tom. Tom opened it slowly, like a prized treasure, and read carefully. It said that Bill never felt right about deserting his daughter and that being in this terrible war made him do a lot of thinking. Seeing the orphaned Vietnamese children made him reconsider his role in Dalia's life, that he didn't want his own child to be an orphan. He decided that when he got back to the states he'd explain to his father how he felt and he was going to make a real home for his daughter, even if his father objected. "Tom, I never showed this letter to my husband. He grieved so much over Bill's death that I just couldn't bear to do it. Maybe I was wrong, but what's done is done."

Neither Tom nor Dorothy spoke for a minute or two. A thousand thoughts ran through Tom's head, he pitied Dorothy and felt her pain.

"Maybe it's time to right the wrong you feel, Dorothy," he said gently.

"Do you think she'd want to see me, Tom?"

"I don't know, Dorothy, I just don't know." Tom went on and explained the circumstances of how he got involved through his friend Frank. He told her his main objective was to find Carrie first, and that Dalia wasn't even sure if she wanted Carrie to know the details and background of what kind of life she'd led the past twenty some years. Dalia was ashamed of what she'd done and how she lived. Tom told Dorothy it was going to be difficult to tell Dalia about Dorothy and Reggie and Bill. "I can't even begin to imagine how she's going to take this all in, Dorothy," Tom said honestly.

"I wouldn't blame her if she doesn't want to see me," Dorothy said, "but I'd like the opportunity to at least tell her about her father and how much he loved her and her mother. I could tell her at least that, Tom, don't you think?" now Dorothy was pleading.

"We'll see," said Tom.

"Oh, please, do what you can, Tom, I would like so much to see my grandbaby after all these years."

They parted ways and Tom couldn't help but feel the burden of Dorothy's mixed emotions, part regret and sadness and shame. It seemed she had lost something she could never regain.

*   *   *   *

At their next breakfast meeting, Tom told Frank about the Robinsons and the facts about Dalia's real father and the fate of him. Daila's early life turned out to be an incredible story, "one for the movies" he said. He related to his friend the near misses, the twists of fate. If only one of them had turned out right, Dalia's life could have been completely different. Both men wondered if and how they should tell Dalia what they knew about her past. They both agreed they would remain silent until they found more information about Carrie. They both hoped that when Carrie was located she'd want to see Dalia as much as Dalia wanted to see her.

CHAPTER 8

▼

It wasn't long after Carrie was sent to St. Mary's Children's Home that Jeremy and Joyce Potter adopted her. Jeremy and Joyce had been married for about ten years and were unable to have children of their own. Jeremy was an engineer at a local manufacturing plant and Joyce was a third grade teacher in the city school district. Carrie was the something that had been missing in their lives. After adopting Carrie, the Potters' happiness was so great, they wanted to share it. So over the next few years, they adopted three more children. When Joyce and Jeremy thought they couldn't be any happier, they were blessed with two children of their own. Carrie thrived in the secure and loving atmosphere of the Potter household. After graduating from high school, she went on to college, and like her adoptive mother, she became an elementary school teacher. While teaching, she met Michael Desmond, a math teacher at the high school. The two were soon married and settled in Albany, NY, where Michael became a high school principal, and Carrie, after taking off six years to raise two daughters and a son, went back to a rewarding career of teaching second grade.

When Carrie got the call from Mr. Rathbone from the Catholic orphanage about someone by the name of "Dalia" wanting to contact her, she was stunned and nearly dropped the phone. She often thought about Dalia, but never mentioned her to her parents or brothers and sisters. There were times when she even wondered if Dalia or Aunt Jesse had ever really existed or had she dreamt them. She often dreamed of meeting Dalia by accident, either on a trip, at school or shopping. One time after she and Michael were married, she told her husband about Aunt Jessie and Dalia, and once they even tried to locate them. However, with limited resources and no knowledge of the location of Aunt Jesse's farm, they were not successful. Carrie had figured that someday when she had more time, or with the help of a private investigator, she would search for her cousin.

Mr. Rathbone told her if she wanted to be contacted, he would give her phone number to a Mr. Tom Dutton, who would set up an appointment for the two women to initially talk by phone. Of course, with Carrie's permission, he emphasized.

Carrie agreed and was overcome by a myriad of feelings, from joy and excitement to fear and guilt. Guilt, because she hadn't truly committed herself to finding Dalia, and she hardly made an effort even to talk about her to her parents. Now, with Mr. Rathbone's request, she was unable to concentrate on anything, her school, her family and friends, because of the overwhelming anticipation of seeing her long lost cousin. Mostly, she was happy, because her dream would soon come true.

*   *   *   *

Tom prepared a written report for Frank about everything he had learned about Dalia's early life. He thought it would be best to document the facts so he wouldn't forget anything, and it would feel more solid in black and white. He also told Frank that Mr. Rathbone contacted Carrie and she was extremely anxious to hear from Dalia.

In the weeks it took Tom to get the information for his report about Dalia, she was completely engrossed in her work at the farm. Steve Wilcox was more than pleased with how quickly she learned. He felt confident giving her more and more responsibilities. She proved herself indeed, he thought. Dalia was a changed woman. Frank's family couldn't believe the progress she had made in just a few weeks. Even though Frank Jr. still had doubts, he was also very impressed. Sharon began to notice a subtle change in her father as well. She noticed that he spoke about Dalia more often and he seemed to arrange his schedule so that he could spend more time with his neighbor. Sharon kept these thoughts to herself, but she was pleased for her father. He seemed genuinely happier than he'd been in a long time.

*   *   *   *

Frank waited until the weekend to give Dalia Tom's report, including the news about her cousin. At first she was excited about getting in touch with Carrie, but then felt embarrassed about her past and was hesitant to finally go through with a formal reunion.

Frank encouraged her to be positive about meeting Carrie after she read Tom's report. He told her that she was a victim of circumstances, and that she would understand that after she read the facts in the report. He left her alone, but told her he'd be just working in the yard if she needed to talk.

Dalia didn't leave her apartment all day. Later that night Frank called on her to see if she wanted anything. Frank remembered when he first saw Dalia at the police station, she had an angry and bitter look about her. Now, she just looked sad and confused. When Dalia opened the door, more than anything else, Frank wanted to put his arms around her and just hold her and comfort her.

"Do you remember any of those times in the report, Dalia?" Frank asked her, after he came in the apartment and she made them a cup of tea.

"No, Frank, it was so confusing. I'm trying to remember things that happened such a long time ago. I don't remember my mother at all. I wish I did. I think I remember the lady that took me to Aunt Jesse's. According to that report, she was my Grandmother, right?" Frank nodded, sipping his tea. "And my Aunt Jesse wasn't really my aunt, at all, so that means Carrie wasn't, isn't, my cousin." She said with disappointment in her voice.

"There's a lot of information in that report, Dalia, and I didn't know how to break it to you all at once. I don't know really what to say, except that I think you are an extraordinary person." He looked down at his feet nervously.

"Me? Extraordinary?"

"Yes, you, Dalia. You've been through so much, and yet look at yourself now. You have a good job, you have a place of your own, and Steve says he can't run the farm market without you. Dalia, the point is, you've come a long way since I first met you."

"Frank, if it wasn't for you, I'd still be on the streets, or who knows where. You don't even know me. You don't know the things I've done. You don't know the people I've been involved with. It ain't pretty either, Frank," she said, half smiling.

"Dalia, what I know about you right now is all I need to know." Frank got up slowly and moved toward her. He took her by the hand and held her close to him. Dalia was never held like that by anyone. She felt comfortable and safe in his strong arms, and wanted to stay there. Then Frank backed away, sliding his hands down the length of her arms to her hands, clasping them tightly, looking at her face. "Now, young lady, what do you want to do about Carrie?"

"I don't know Frank," she whispered, nearly in tears. She put her head on his shoulder and they stood there silently for a short while.

"I have a friend who lives in Albany that I haven't seen in a while. Maybe we could drive up there together and I could pay my friend a visit, while you visit Carrie?" She looked at him, saying nothing. "How 'bout it? Dalia, I think you owe it to yourself to see her. If you and Carrie were as close as you say you were as children, I'm sure she wants to see you as much as you want to see her."

"But, Frank, what do I say when she or her family asks what I've been doing all these years? Can I just blurt out that I've been addicted to drugs and a prostitute who stole and conned for a living? That some nights I begged and panhandled just to get by? That there were days when I was so strung out that I didn't even know how I got into all kinds of messes and situations? How do I get around *that*, Frank?" Dalia pleaded.

"Dalia, one of the things that impressed me the most about you in Tom's report, was the part about how you got your name. Do you remember that? That phrase, 'D' ha lal liah' is *you*. Rosetta gave you that name and the attributes of *strength*, *determination*, *strong will to survive*, and the one that's important to you now, *flourish*.

Dalia, that inner spirit that you had all those years got you through the worst part of your life. And now you *can* flourish. Dalia, you have what it takes to survive under the worst conditions, and now it's your turn to thrive and flourish. Dalia, be proud of yourself. Like I said, you've come a long way in such a short time. Forget the past, because that's what it is, passed. From this point on you can do what you want and be who you want to be."

"I don't know, Frank, you sound so sure. I owe you so much. You make me feel so right."

Frank extended his arms and Dalia walked to him. With a gentle embrace they said good night.

*   *   *   *

Maria Vargas arrived at her office early that morning. She had a lot of work to catch up on and she knew that she accomplished more when no one else was around to disturb her. She was startled when she heard a knock on her door. It was still before hours and most of her colleagues didn't arrive until after nine. A second knock, harder this time and she wondered who it could be.

Working in the inner city neighborhoods where most of her clients were from, Maria was never really scared for her safety. She never felt threatened, and she was always cautious, alert and aware of her surroundings at all times. However, when she opened the door and saw Baxter standing there in his black leather trench coat and fedora hat low on his head, she was gripped by an unmistakable fear. She did her best not to show it, but she knew her voice gave her away. This was the third or fourth time he had been in to see Maria to find out about Dalia and where she was staying.

"Baxter, it's you," she said shakily, trying to conceal the nervousness in her words. "What are you doing here so early, not even my co-workers are here yet."

"Oh, Miss Maria, I just came by to tell you how concerned I am about my Dalia. I miss her so much, you can't imagine.

None of my other girls can take Dalia's place, you know that," he said sarcastically

"Baxter, now, now," Maria said, trying to speak soothingly, "you know you should just forgot about Dalia. As far as I know, nobody knows where she is."

"Maria, I know you better than that, give me some credit. I'm not as dumb as you look. You know that's a bold faced lie, and you know I'll find her. I always have." He stepped closer to her, "And you know she'll come with me when I do, so why don't you make it easy for her. Or haven't you heard how angry I get when one of my women tries to stray," Baxter said slowly, closer now to her face, tapping her on the chin.

Maria backed away, went over to her desk. "Baxter, can't you let it go? You have so many others."

"Never, senorita!" raising his voice, "The only way I would let her go is if you join me, how 'bout it, bitch?" He leaned across the desk and grabbed her wrists, pulled her to him and said, "I can use a spunky old lady like you."

"Let me go, I'll have you arrested," she yelled back, yanking away from him and smoothing down her dress.

"Just think about what I said, make it easy on her and yourself. I won't be so nice next time," he said, as he tightened the belt of his coat, tipped his hat, and walked slowly out the door.

Maria stood stunned, motionless; she didn't know what to do. She knew Baxter didn't make idle threats, and she knew that if he did find Dalia, he'd be tough with her, more than tough. Maybe not right away, but she knew his reputation. She feared for Frank too. The world of a pimp and his women had a code all its own. The rules were strict and the punishment for a transgression was brutal.

*   *   *   *

Frank and Dalia couldn't have picked a more perfect day for their trip to Albany. The sun was bright and the air crisp as they started out early that autumn morning. They planned to drive for an hour, then stop for breakfast at a country diner that Frank knew in the area. Frank couldn't help but notice how nice Dalia looked. She wore a red dress with a white blazer and a single strand of beads around her neck. She had been out with Sharon a few times to do some shopping to work on her wardrobe, and it definitely showed Dalia had a natural sense of style.

This was the first time that they had been out alone together and Frank felt like it was a date. Since a few nights ago when they embraced, Frank kept thinking how good it felt to hold Dalia. He began to feel differently towards her, but was embarrassed when he realized he was old enough to be her father. It's just a harmless crush, he told himself, and hoped Dalia didn't recognize any change in his feelings or actions. He didn't want anything to upset or make her uncomfortable, at least not today of all days.

Dalia was anxious to see Carrie since their last phone call. As soon as she heard her voice, any doubts Dalia had about Carrie's opinion of her past, were quickly dismissed. Her eyes sparkled at the thought of seeing her long lost "cousin." Carrie had told Dalia that her husband, Michael, would be busy with their son at a soccer tournament, and her two daughters would be on a camping trip with some friends. They would have plenty of time to reminisce about the old times with Aunt Jesse.

When Frank pulled up in the driveway of Carrie's house, even though Dalia was excited to see her, he sensed her apprehension and nervousness. He reached over, took her hand and squeezed it. "You're going to be okay," he said.

"I know, I will. Thank you for everything," Dalia said meeting his eyes, then looking away quickly.

Carrie met Dalia half way up the stone walkway. Frank watched as the two women hugged and kissed. He heard cries of joy and laughter, and knew everything was going as he expected.

Carrie and Dalia's reunion brought more joy to Dalia than she imagined. Memories surfaced so vivid and so fast, that both women had a hard time keeping up with one another. Tears, hugs, and laughter constantly interrupted the conversation. They acted and sounded like the seven-year-olds they were so many years ago. They suddenly turned into the same little girls who tried to smother their giggles under the covers in their bedroom, so Aunt Jesse wouldn't hear them in the next room. The same girls who laughed every time the Reverend at church squealed like a pig when reached the high notes at choir practice; and the same girls who swapped ice cream cones using just their tongues.

Finally Dalia said, "Carrie, I missed you so much. When we first separated, I always hoped and prayed I would see you the next day. And then maybe the next day, but that day never came. I wanted to see you and be with you again so much."

"Dalia, I don't know what to say. I wish I could've been with you. I was so scared, I think we both didn't know what to do."

"Carrie, we were only kids, there was nothing either one of us could've done. I know that now. Up until a few days ago, I didn't know if I wanted you to know about me. I was quite different from the girl you remembered at Aunt Jessie's. I was ashamed of who I was and the things I've done. Carrie, when I heard your voice on the phone, all I wanted was to see you again and hug you. Somehow, I knew that whatever I had been or whatever I had done, wouldn't have mattered to you. You always were nice and kind to me. You and Aunt Jesse were the only two people I could trust."

"Oh, Dalia, the only thing that matters now is that we're together, and nothing will ever separate us again. I can't wait until you meet my family. They'll love you just like I do." She put her arms around Dalia and hugged her so hard, she thought she'd break a rib.

*   *   *   *

As planned, Frank went over to Carrie's early the next morning to pick up Dalia. He met Carrie and her family, and after a pleasant visit and some light refreshments, Dalia and Frank left to return to Oakdale.

On the way home they decided to stop and have something to eat at a restaurant. While they sat at a booth waiting for their order, they noticed a couple that were dining a few tables over and had looked at them a few times. Dalia was used to getting stares, but Frank was not.

"They must be commenting on the old guy with the good looking young woman," Frank said to Dalia.

Dalia smiled, gestured with her hand, "Forget them," she said, waving them off.

A few minutes later music started playing, and Frank said, "Let's give them something to really look at," taking Dalia's hand and leading her to the dance floor. Although Dalia was not familiar with the kind of music playing or the dance moves, she felt comfortable with Frank as he led her around the dance floor, her hand nestled in his. Frank held her close, enjoying the scent of her perfume, feeling her body move with his. He hoped he wasn't making a fool of himself. As the dance ended, they both knew they were becoming more than friends. Dalia noticed they were the only couple still on the floor when the music stopped. She laughed nervously as she let go of Frank's hand.

"Our food's here," she said softly, as they walked back to their booth.

That night when Frank dropped her off and walked her to the door of the apartment, he hesitated to leave. "I enjoyed this day with you, Dalia, and I hope you don't think I'm being presumptuous, but I'd like to go out with you again, maybe dinner and a movie," he said.

"Are you asking me out, Frank?" Dalia said.

"Yes, I think I am," he said shyly.

"Well, Frank, since I've never really been asked out on a real date before, I think I'll accept." Frank beamed and leaned over and kissed her on the cheek.

"Good night, Dalia," he said.

"Good night, Frank. I'll see you tomorrow," she said.

As Frank walked along the path to his front door on the other side of the driveway, he wondered if he should've kissed her again, the second time a real kiss on the mouth. He wanted to, but felt foolish, then felt even more foolish second guessing himself like a kid. All he knew was that he liked Dalia very much, very much indeed.

Dalia couldn't believe this was happening to her. Was she falling in love? Was this feeling even love? She felt strange, but in a good way. All she knew was that she was very, very happy for the first time in many, many years.

Just before Frank retired for the night, he sat on the edge of the bed and looked at Laura's picture, like he did many times. As if he were asking her permission, he lifted the tiny frame and said, "I hope you don't mind, Laura, but I like this woman. I like being with her, and she makes me feel good. You know you will always be the number one in my heart, and no one can ever take your place, but these last few weeks I've felt whole again. I look forward to seeing her and I enjoy our time together in the garden, just talking about the events of the day, like you and I did so often, Laura. I feel that you had something to do with this whole episode of my life, and I don't know how or why, but I feel it and I'm never been wrong about a feeling when it comes to you. You remember, don't you?" he said as he lifted the picture and kissed it. "I'll love you forever, my darling. We'll always be as close as we always were. Thank you, and good night, Laura."

Baxter was extremely frustrated and angry not being able to get any information on Dalia's whereabouts. It was true he really didn't need her, but he couldn't let any of his friends know that he was giving up on her so easily. Besides, Dalia was a cash cow for him. She not only worked the streets, but she couldn't stay away from the drugs he supplied. He'd be a living idiot to forget about her, and giving up would send the wrong message to his other women and the competing pimps.

Baxter decided that he would put a price on Dalia's head. He'd have someone else do his dirty work. He put word out on the streets that he would pay a handsome reward to anyone who gave him information on where she was. Although Baxter couldn't be trusted even amongst his degenerate friends, he knew that if anyone knew anything about Dalia, they'd come forward because they feared what might happen if they didn't.

*   *   *   *

Johnny "Short Shoes" Lewis lived in the neighborhood for a long time. He was a likeable guy with a perpetual smile and a gift for gab. He got his nickname from when he was a boy and had to wear the same pair of shoes even though he had out-grown them. He used to cut out the toes so you could see his socks sticking out. Even today, he still cut out the front of his sneakers. Johnny was a "wannabe." He was not a pimp, not a drug pusher, not a criminal, but he liked to hang around them, and be part of the rough crowd. Johnny spent some time in prison when he was younger for stealing a car once, so he did his best to stay out of trouble and keep clean and quiet. Whenever he needed money he'd go down to the local day labor office and work a day or two here and there, get his money, and then hang around the streets until he needed some more cash.

One morning, when Johnny went to apply at the labor office, he was told about a job on a farm near Oakdale that needed a few men. Johnny was not crazy about farm work, too many bugs and your hands got dirty, but it paid well and he thought the change of scenery and some fresh country air might be good for him.

Johnny had known Dalia from the neighborhood and had liked her, but had to be careful around her because she was one of Baxter's favorites. If he was suspected of even looking at her too often or just too long, he could get into a heap of trouble. Also if Dalia looked at Johnny or any other man for that fact, who was not a "john," she could get into a lot of trouble too. It was nothing to see one of the girls get a beating by her pimp and the pimps liked to slap their women around for show. It was a cruel game, and Johnny always felt sorry for the girls, but there was little he could do in his position.

*   *   *   *

Dalia was practically Steve Wilcox's right hand man at this time. He could depend on her to do almost any job. Dalia was busy at the market that morning setting up a fresh display of apples, peaches, cauliflower, and all kinds of squash. Steve marveled at her handiwork and had more time to do office work, running a more efficient business. A few minutes later he received a phone call and had to leave for a short time to run an errand. He asked Dalia if she would ride out with his driver, Sam, to show the pickers where to start work that morning in the fields. Dalia, agreeable as usual, set aside her immediate task and accompanied Sam to the fields. When they arrived, Sam assembled the twelve or so men while Dalia explained how and where to pick and urged them to be careful, not to bruise the produce.

As she walked way, Johnny "Short Shoes" thought he recognized her. Dalia's appearance was always striking, and she looked very different than when she was on the streets, but her beautiful eyes gave her away.

"What's that lady's name?" Johnny asked Tony, one of the regular farm hands.

"That's Steve's best worker, Dolly or something like that. Why do you ask?" Tony grumbled back.

"Oh, nothing, I just thought I knew her or something," Johnny responded, he didn't want to let on that he recognized Dalia. He was sure it was her, however, and she was on his mind all day. He wanted to find out how much the reward was before he told anyone he had seen her.

The next day Johnny sought out Baxter to tell him he might know where Dalia was. Johnny never liked Baxter, thought he was a mean son of a bitch, and it crossed his mind that maybe he wouldn't even bother to tell him. But with his back aching from all the apple picking he had done the previous day, he figured the bit of news might be worth a hundred dollars or more, easy. After all, Dalia was one of Baxter's favorites, and he really wanted her back, and it's been such a long time that she's been gone. "Oh, yes," Johnny thought out loud, "this is going to be 'easy money'!"

After he announced that he had some information for Baxter, Baxter sent out word that he wanted to see Johnny. Baxter was in the back room of a local bar with a few of his women plus two other pimps and their women, enjoying a drink and some honest poker playing. Johnny felt a bit uneasy and asked if he could see Baxter in private.

"Any information you have, fool, you can tell me in front of my friends," Baxter responded to his request.

"I might have some information about a certain person you might be looking for," Johnny said.

"Is that right?"

"Yes, sir," Johnny answered nervously, not knowing Baxter's reaction.

"Well, you go ahead, man, what do you know?"

"Well, Baxter, I was kind of wondering about the … uh…. you know …"

"The *what*, asshole?" Baxter cut him off. The room got quiet, all eyes on Baxter and Johnny. "What information, I repeat. You haven't told me a damn thing so far. Now, speak up man, what do you know?" Baxter bellowed.

"Yyyyyyyou know," Johnny stuttered, "your friend Dalia."

"Dalia? You mean my baby, Dalia? Shit, man, I know where she is. Did you think I needed you to find her? And just so you know, I can't believe you would betray her like that. I thought you liked her, Johnny. Do you have any idea what she's in for now?"

"But how did you find out?" Johnny stammered in disbelief.

"Don't you know that I know where you went yesterday? Don't you think I put two and two together? Do you think I'm as dumb as you are, fool?" Baxter yelled.

"Well, how about the reward, then?"

"Reward? Here's your reward," and in a flash Baxter came across the room and swung the back of his hand across Johnny's face, knocking him to the floor.

"But I found her," Johnny whispered, "I saw her first."

"Go buy yourself a pair of shoes, rat," Baxter snickered as he threw a crumpled ten dollar bill at Johnny's feet.

As the crowded dispersed, Johnny lay there with the ten dollars in his hand. His nose was bleeding and he ached terribly. He got himself up and shook his clothes off, shuffled to his feet, and walked out of the room, shaking his head. "You'll get yours, Baxter," he said under his breath as he walked out and threw the crumpled bill on the floor.

*   *   *   *

As Frank dressed for his date with Dalia, he started to doubt whether he was doing the right thing. What would his friends and family think about his dating a woman young enough to be his daughter? And then there was the race issue. It didn't matter to him, but he knew even today there would still be talk. After all, the couple that looked at them in the restaurant the other night on their way home from Albany was not the exception. "Oh, forget it," Frank said out loud as he put on his sport jacket. He was simply taking a friend out to dinner and the theatre. "Why am I making such a fuss?" No matter what he said to himself, this was a special evening, no denying that.

Frank had dated a couple of times since Laura's death, but on those occasions he almost had to force himself to go out. Those times he couldn't help but think of his wife, as if he was cheating on her, and that's why he was so reluctant to date. However, this was different. He was looking forward to seeing Dalia this evening. He felt that Laura approved and that's why he was excited and didn't feel any guilt.

*   *   *   *

Across the yard, strange things were going through Dalia's mind as she prepared for her date with Frank. This was a new experience for her. She was concerned about what she wore, her hair, the perfume, everything. She wished she had someone to call for advice or just discuss "girl stuff." The only two people she was close to were Sharon and Maria Vargas. What would either of them say if she told them about her date with Frank and her feelings for him. "Maybe I should've refused tonight," she thought. "What is his family going to think of me, a woman young enough to be his daughter. What will Sharon say? She's been so good to me. And I can hear Maria now, 'Child! Are you out of your mind? Do you want to ruin the only good thing that's happened to you in your life?' Maybe I am crazy, she thought. "But I do like being with him, it just feels right. It will probably only be for tonight anyway. Why would someone like Frank want to be with me ... an ex-hooker and drug addict? I'm sure there are plenty of women he'd prefer and his family would approve of. I'm just going to enjoy myself tonight and be happy for this special time."

Frank felt like a schoolboy on his first date as he walked across the yard to Dalia's apartment. He straightened his tie and knocked on her door. On the other side, Dalia held her breath as she opened the door and welcomed Frank in. As they stood and greeted each other you couldn't find a happier couple at that exact moment in time.

*   *   *   *

At dinner they talked about everything under the sun. He told her how he used to be picked on at school, that his mother made him eat eggplant which he detested, that his sister got into a terrible car accident when she was in her late teens and almost didn't make it. "If it wasn't for my faith," he told Dalia, "I would've gone to the funny farm. It was a tough time in my life. Speaking of farms," he added, "how's work?" Frank loved listening to Dalia about what was happening at the farm market, the harvest, and how happy she was to be able to work in the country.

"I am truly grateful, Frank," she said, "to everyone who helped me get to this point in my life. Sometimes I think I'm dreaming and that I'll wake up and the dream will be over."

"It's not a dream, Dalia," Frank assured her. "You can live your life this way for as long as you want to. Only you are in control of your own destiny now."

After they shared a few laughs at the playhouse by the local theatre group, they stopped for a drink to listen to some music at a nearby nightclub. Again, they danced. Some slow dances and some up beat, but they especially enjoyed the slow dances and felt comfortable in each other's arms. When the last song stopped, Frank pulled away and stared into Dalia's eyes. "You know," he said, "I never told you, but you have the most beautiful eyes I've ever seen."

"Why, thank you, Frank," she said shyly, looking down nervously.

"No, Dalia, I mean that, you are a beautiful woman, not only on the outside, but in here," he said, pointing to her heart.

"No one has ever said that to me before," she said, and leaned toward him and kissed him on the mouth. "Thank you Frank for this, for allowing me to feel again."

"No, thank *you*," he said. They held hands as they walked back to their table.

When Frank walked Dalia to her apartment that night, he took her hand and gave her a tender kiss. "We've crossed the line, you know," he said. They both stopped at her door.

"I know," she said, opening the door, and motioned him to come in. When they were inside, alone and in the dark except for the moonlight outside the window, they embraced and kissed again. She was soft and warm. He felt feelings he thought he had abandoned years ago. He held the back of her head, felt her strong cheekbones against his face and got excited. They were in love, no question. From this point on their lives would never be the same.

＊   ＊   ＊   ＊

One evening when Dalia got home after work, she took a shower and changed. She knew that Frank wouldn't be home too early because he had mentioned he was playing in a golf tournament with his son Frank Jr. Since their date Dalia looked forward to spending the evenings with Frank sitting in the yard on these cool fall evenings.

It surprised and excited her then when she heard a car drive up, and then a knock at her door. Assuming it was Frank, she didn't worry that she still had her bathrobe on, and didn't hesitate to open the door. Dalia was speechless and terrified when she saw Baxter standing before her. She began to tremble when he looked at her with a wicked smile and said, "My, oh, my, don't you look good! You're shaking, baby, you mean you're that excited to see me?" as he brushed his hand across her cheek seductively. He stepped forward while Dalia backed away. "C'mon now, girl, that's not nice. That's no way to treat your man." He reached out with his arm and took her around the waist, pulling her toward him and planting a kiss on her mouth. Dalia pulled away, then noticed the door was still opened. Suddenly she realized that Frank would be home and might see her with Baxter. When she got to the door, she had the urge to run outside, but realized she wouldn't get very far and she didn't want Frank to see her running from Baxter. "What could he do?" she thought, "Baxter was a powerful man." Frank was no match for him.

Dalia closed the door and spoke for the first time.

"What do you want, Baxter?" her voice barely audible.

"I just wanted to see you, baby," he said sweetly. "I just missed you so much. After all, you know how much you mean to me." His words dripping with sarcasm. He looked around the room. "You sure have a nice place here. I kinda like it. I think I could be very comfortable here. You know, Dalia, we can set up shop, so to speak," he laughed, "right here under this little roof. Yes, I think it has possibilities. Or maybe you'd like to come back to the city. You're old friends really miss you," he coaxed. "You know, your *special* friends, remember them? When I told them I'd be bringing you home tonight, they really got excited. So … what do you think? It shouldn't take too long for you to get ready, huh?"

Dalia was so frightened she could hardly think straight. She couldn't leave here with Baxter, she thought. How was she going to escape him? His looks, his smell, his demeanor, the repulsive life he led, no way could she ever go back to that. She'd rather die. Dalia was dizzy with thought. She wanted him to leave soon before Frank came home.

"I can't leave with you today, Baxter," she said calmly. "I have obligations. I'll come back to the city this weekend, Saturday. I'll take care of everything and see you on Saturday, okay?" She tried to hide her nervousness, and started to straighten up the coffee table and walked distractedly around the furniture. "That was my plan anyway," she said fluffing up a pillow, throwing it back on the sofa. "There's nothing keeping me here, I'll see you on Saturday," she repeated.

"Saturday? I can't wait that long," Baxter whined. "No, it's got to be tonight, girl." He stepped closer to her, invading her private space. "My goodness with the way you look, I can't wait to get my arms around you and …" Baxter grabbed her arm and tried to kiss her again. She moved back, but he was stronger and held her tightly around the waist. "If I didn't know you better, I'd think you weren't very happy to see me right now." Dalia tried to get away, but his hold was gripping, she could hardly move.

Just then they heard a knock at the door. Dalia was petrified. Please don't let it be Frank, she thought to herself. She didn't want him to see Baxter here, not now, not now, she panicked.

Frank slowly pushed open the door and saw Dalia and a tall black man. He was completely taken by surprised. He could feel his face drop. He had absolutely no idea who this man was and why he was in Dalia's apartment with his hand around

Dalia's wrist. Could it be an intruder who followed her home and forced his way in? Someone from the farm market? Why does he have her by the arm like that? He was puzzled and tried to process and make sense out of the scene in front of him.

His first reaction was to rush in and take Dalia by the other arm and pull her out of danger. As he started to make a move toward her, Baxter said in a loud, forceful voice, "Be careful, old man, you don't want to do anything you'll be sorry for."

As Frank continued forward, he heard a familiar voice coming from the pathway. It was Frank, Jr. After dropping his dad off, he realized his father left his golf shoes in his car. As he drove in the driveway, he saw that something was not right through the window and he didn't recognize the car parked in the driveway of his Dad's house. On his cell phone he called 9–1–1.

As Frank Jr. neared the apartment, he said slowly, "Everyone stay calm, I just called the police and they'll be here shortly to settle whatever's going on here."

Baxter, sensing things weren't going as smoothly for him, let go of Dalia's arm. "Don't worry, bitch, you haven't seen the last of me." He hurried out of the apartment, brushing Frank against the shoulder. Frank started to follow him, but Frank Jr. stopped him, "Let him go, Dad, just let him go." Frank looked at his father's eyes and knew Dalia meant more to him than just a friend. He wondered and worried what would happen next.

"What's going on, Dad?" Frank, Jr. asked.

"I don't know, son," Frank replied. "I got here just before you did. I saw the strange car and wondered whose it was. I wanted to check in on Dalia, when I heard a man's voice, and thought Dalia was having some sort of problem, so I walked to the door and heard her say that she couldn't leave with him today. That's when I walked in. Within a few minutes I heard you and thought 'thank God' someone called the police."

"Where's Dalia now?"

"She's in her room. She's embarrassed, and a little scared, I think. I don't know the whole story."

Dad, I'd like to wait until the police come, but I have to leave soon for a meeting. I'm worried about you, that's all," Frank Jr. said, as he patted his Dad on the back.

"I know, son, I understand," Frank said in return, giving his son a hug.

Shortly the police arrived and started to gather information by asking questions and filling out a report. Dalia came out of her room, her eyes swollen and red, part exhaustion and part angry and upset. She told the officer that Baxter did not strike her, but grabbed her and left marks on her arms and wrist. Dalia didn't know if Baxter was his first or last name, he was always just Baxter to her. She felt awkward trying to explain her relationship to him, and didn't know how he found her in the first place. The officer explained that he couldn't do much, especially if he didn't strike her. Baxter couldn't be charged with assault, and there was no guarantee he wouldn't come back.

Dalia's expression was one of anger and confusion, the same look Frank remembered when he first saw her at the police station so many months ago. It seemed strange to see her this way, after so many positive changes in her life. This was a major setback.

After the officer left, Dalia broke down and cried uncontrollably. Frank went to her on the sofa, lifted her face in his hands, held her and looked into her eyes. "Everything is going to be okay, Dalia. I'll take care of everything, you'll see," he said confidently. She sobbed even harder and lost herself in his chest, wishing she could disappear.

*   *   *   *

While Dalia regained her composure, Frank had made a pot of coffee and Dalia was ready to talk.

"Frank, things will not be okay. You don't know this man, and what he can do.

I'm going to have to leave the apartment, the job, because now that Baxter knows where I live, the man won't rest until I'm back with him."

"What do you mean, until you're back with him?" Frank asked. "You don't have to go back anywhere."

"Frank, you don't understand. You don't know anything. I should have known that this would happen. Remember when I told you that sometimes I think I'm dreaming, that this is too good to be true, you, the apartment, the job? Well, that's what it's been, just a dream and now I'm awake to the reality."

"Dalia, what are you talking about? Forget about this Baxter, he can't make you do anything you don't want to do. As far as I know, this is still a free county."

"Frank, I told you before, you don't know anything about me, I'm a whore, a prostitute, a streetwalker … use any term you like. That's what I am. Baxter is my pimp. He owns me. He provides a place for me to stay, he buys me clothes, he tells me where and when to work and what to charge. Then when I'm feeling down and I'm so disgusted with myself that I can't even bear to look at myself in the mirror, he gives me something to forget. How do you think I got my drugs? And I owe him that, Frank, and I owe him a lot, because I haven't been able to stand myself for a long, long time." Dalia stopped talking, and rested her head across her folded arms on the table. She wanted to sleep and forget everything.

"Stop talking like that, Dalia, I don't want to hear it, you hear me?" Frank said. "Tomorrow I'll go to the authorities and get a restraining order and he won't be able to come back here again. You hear me, Dalia, sweetheart?" He nudged her, wanting to see her face. "I don't care what you were before we met, you are the woman I love now, and that's that."

"Frank," Dalia lifted her head, "Frank you don't hear what I'm saying. Baxter is a pimp, a man of the streets, a hardcore, mean man. He'll find me. And what about the farm market, Frank, are you going to keep him away from there too? I don't think so." Dalia's tone of voice changed, as if she had already given up and didn't even hear Frank's profession of love he just spoke. "Frank, honey," she extended her arm and cradled his hands in hers. "It's useless. People like Baxter don't pay attention to laws. They have a way around them. They only follow the laws of the street. And the only thing that Baxter is interested in now, is to get me back so he can make an example of me. He'll show his other whores that nobody gets away from him without paying the price. Nobody!" she shouted, pointing a finger in the air.

"Dalia, you're upset now, and you have the right to be, but I won't let anyone take you from me, not now, Dalia. When I first met you I just wanted to help you out, get you on your feet. But now you mean too much to me, I don't think I can go on without you. You're a part of me now. When I first lost my wife I didn't want to go on, but I did. I went through the motions. Let's just say, I existed. I had to, there was my family, my work and friends. But in the last few weeks, Dalia, I've realized why I survived those first few years alone. I was searching for a reason to go on. I didn't know what that reason would be, but now I know the reason is you. When Laura got sick, she was taken from me, and no matter how I tried there was nothing I could do to keep her, absolutely nothing. I couldn't fight a disease. But Baxter is not a disease, and I love you too much and nobody will take you from me. The only way you can go is if you want to."

"Frank, I don't know, I just don't know," she cried, and fell into his arms.

*   *   *   *

Later when Dalia was alone, she thought how much Frank had done for her. She thought about him and how important he was to his family and his family to him. She thought about how much he must have hurt when he lost his wife. He was a man that has loved without reservation, unconditionally. He was a man who was loved and respected by his family and friends. Frank brought her into a world that she never knew existed. He made her realize that if it wasn't for some peculiar set of circumstances, she could've been truly loved by her mother and father and the rest of her family and friends. He brought her together with Carrie, who was the only family she had known. He had shown her that she was a person who could be of value to her self, her friends, and to society. Above all, she realized that Frank taught her how to love and what true love is. She could never repay him for what he had given her. And Frank would never expect anything nor want anything from her.

At that moment Dalia realized she truly loved this man more than anything or anyone. But where could their love go? Could they marry? Live together? Be lovers? That wasn't Frank, despite his statements of love and taking care of everything. No, it wouldn't work. She was in too deep with Baxter's world, and getting Frank involved in it would only lead to trouble. No way would Frank be able to deal with the Baxters of the world. Frank didn't deserve the grief she knew Baxter would cause him. She must do something, but what? Then she remembered when Frank said that the only way she could leave is if she *wanted* to.

*   *   *   *

That night Frank planned on how he was going to handle the problem. First he'd go to the police and make sure Baxter didn't go to the apartment or the farm market. Then he'd go see Maria Vargas to see if she couldn't set up some kind of contact with Baxter to see what it would take to leave Dalia alone. He felt confident that he could handle the situation.

Frank got up early that morning to see Dalia so he could comfort her, and tell her that he had worked out a plan and things would be okay. "Don't worry, darling," he said, smoothing down her hair and rubbing her cheeks.

"Thank you, Frank," Dalia said calmly. "I know everything will be okay, too." Frank was a little surprised at how relaxed and assured she was after being so frantic the night before, but he felt good she had a change of heart. They embraced and kissed before Frank left to run some errands in the city, saying he'd not be gone long.

While driving back home, he thought how calm and relaxed Dalia was that morning, and he began to wonder why. He decided to stop by the farm market to see her before he went to the City, just to see if she was still as encouraged and focused. He was surprised to see that she hadn't been to work yet. He was actually quite alarmed, and decided to go back to the apartment to see what happened.

As he drove up the driveway, he noticed Baxter's car. He became very angry at himself for not staying with her that morning. He should've trusted his intuition, he thought. As Frank rushed up the walkway, the door opened and he couldn't believe his eyes. Baxter and Dalia were leaving together. She had a suitcase, and a coat swung over her arm.

"What's going on here?" he asked. "What do you think you're doing?" He shouted at Baxter. "She's not going anywhere with you. You can't take her." As Frank stepped forward, Dalia got between the two men.

"Frank, it's not what you think. I called him, it's my choice. I want to leave," she said matter-of-factly.

"I don't believe it," Frank said.

"Please believe it, Frank, I explained everything to you in a letter over there," as she pointed behind her on the kitchen table. "This is the best way for now," she said.

"Dalia, you don't have to go with him, I'm going to take care of everything, I told you." Frank pleaded. Baxter was getting impatient.

"C'mon, let's get going, forget it, old man. If you want anymore of her you can come downtown and pay for it like the rest of her customers," Baxter said snidely and grabbed Dalia by the arm and pulled her away.

"Get your hands off of her," Frank demanded. He went forward and reached for Dalia. Instantly, Baxter struck Frank across the upper arm, but was met with more resistance than he anticipated, coming from a man of Frank's size and age. As Frank moved forward, directing a closed fist to Baxter's face, Baxter struck him first with a short but powerful punch to Frank's midsection. Frank gasped and then appeared motionless as if trying to catch his breath, then fell to the floor. In the midst of the confrontation, Dalia was pushed away and landed on the sofa. As Frank lay huddled on the floor, she noticed his bloodied shirt, then realized Baxter had a knife in his hand when he delivered the blow beneath Frank's heart. She immediately got hysterical, as she knelt to the floor and cradled

Frank's lifeless body in her arms, gently rocking him, scream-ing, **NO, NO, NO, GOD, NO, NO!"**

*   *   *   *

Baxter was caught a short time later while he was trying to gather enough money to get out of town. He is now serving 25 years to life in a maximum security State prison. Most of the people in the neighborhood are glad to see him gone. And the rest just don't care.

*   *   *   *

Frank's funeral was one of the largest in the area. People came from all over to pay their respects, and both family and friends eulogized him. People were shocked by how he was killed. An unfortunate accident that nobody seemed to under-stand. And that woman who lived in Frank's garden apart-ment, what was she all about? There would always be talk. Dalia took a cab to the cemetery and remained far enough away from the crowd so no one would see her. She felt, how-ever, that she had to be there, to pay her last final respects to the man who gave her a second chance.

*   *   *   *

Dalia was hospitalized for a short time after the incident, and treated for shock and depression. Eventually she made a complete recovery, and moved into a small apartment near

Marley and worked at a nearby flower shop. Her life was quite different from what it was a year before.

The tragedy of what happened that fateful morning would always be with her. As the memory of what Frank meant to her would never go away. The short time they knew each other was one of the happiest times of her life.

Epilogue

▼

As Sharon got closer to the city, thoughts and feelings about her father overwhelmed her. Would it have been better if her father had never got involved with Dalia? He would still be alive, his family would still have him. Was the happiness he had with Dalia for that short time worth his getting killed, and the pain that his family is having now? Life goes on. Eventually the hurt will become less and less. Time has a way of doing that. The lives that were touched by that encounter will get back to normal, or will they?

Baxter can no longer abuse the women or the people around him. Maria Vargas will continue to try and help people against all odds.

When Sharon got back to the city later that day she called Maria Vargas to tell her about her visit with Dalia. They agreed to meet over lunch the following day.

The two women hadn't seen each other in almost a year. Maria was delighted to hear about Dalia's new life and the difference she was making in her small community. She liked the idea she was helping her new boss not only in his business, but personally by taking care of him.

While Sharon sat and shared news about Dalia and herself, Maria sensed the mixed emotions her friend must have felt. On the one hand she was happy that Dalia turned her life around and was becoming a successful business woman, but she also couldn't get over the fact that Dalia's new life had come at the expense of her father's life. Maria reached across the table and took Sharon's hand, "Sharon, there's nothing that I can say that can make the pain of your father's sacrifice go away. I cannot imagine how you feel. Your father was such a special man. I never knew a man like him before, and I'll probably never know one like him again. You were so fortunate to have him as a father. Sharon, that's what you have to focus on. Not the loss you feel, but the joy and happiness you had growing up in a home where you were nurtured, loved, and respected. Sharon, I see first hand every day the abuse, pain and suffering that people, especially family members cause each other."

"I know, Maria, I know," Sharon said, as she wiped the beginning flow of tears on her face.

"Before I met your father, I thought people like you were only imagined, only in the movies. Your father is an inspiration to me, and his memory makes me get up every morning, believe it or not, and do my job with the hope that maybe I can make a difference in someone's life. I want to rescue one person, just one person from the hopelessness and despair that surrounds them. Sharon, you'll hurt less and less as time goes on, and then the joy and pride of your father's accomplishments will flood your memory," Maria said and reached out her hands across the table for Sharon to hold. "Your father is in a better place now, I know you believe that. I do."

"Yes, Maria, I do. I know he is in a better place. After all, he's with my mother."

Sharon and Maria got up slowly, embraced and then promised each other they'd keep in touch at least a couple times a year. It was more difficult to say good-by to Maria than Sharon expected, and Maria felt likewise. They had crossed each other's paths, worlds apart, and yet filled with the same restless longing, searching for an ideal, something they couldn't quite capture or create, which made them connected in every sense of the word.

*   *   *   *

The last thing Sharon thought about as she lay in bed that night were Maria's words "Your father is in a better place now." The words comforted her as she drifted off to sleep.

There is a beautiful woman sitting on a bench in a lovely garden, smiling peacefully at the flowers before her. By the look on her face you can tell she is very happy and content. A handsome man approaches her from the right, she turns and looks at him. She is pleasantly surprised and she lifts her hands for him to take hold of. They look at each other for an instant, then embrace.

They hold each other that way for a long, long time. Frank and Laura together again.

The End

978-0-595-42239-5
0-595-42239-X

Printed in the United States
201282BV00001B/1-18/P

9 780595 422395